WHO LIES INSIDE

Timothy Ireland was born in Southborough, Kent in 1959 and now lives and works in London. His previous publications include the novels *Catherine Loves* and *To Be Looked For*.

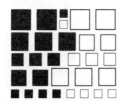

TIMOTHY IRELAND
WHO LIES INSIDE

First published in May 1984 by GMP Publishers Ltd,
    P O Box 247, London N15 6RW
2nd impression 1985

Distributed in North America by Alyson Publications Inc.,
    40 Plympton St, Boston, MA 02118

British Library Cataloguing in Publication Data
            Ireland, Timothy
                Who lies inside.
                I. Title
                823'.914/F/   PR6059.R4/

                ISBN 0-907040-30-6

Cover art by Graham Ward
Printed and bound by Billing & Sons Ltd, Worcester

to
MILES PARKER
and
Jack, for his kindness
David Fleckney, despite silence
and Rosalyn Connor and her Green Bed.
This is also for Mum and Dad,
my family and friends.

I suppose, first of all, I should tell you my name. It's Martin Conway. From the outside I look just like an ordinary young man, though perhaps I'm a bit taller than most. My friends in the rugby team at school call me Jumbo. It's my nickname. I don't mind it, not really ... You might see someone like me on any street in any town, walking along not too sure of myself, a tall, well-built young man in jumper and jeans. But inside something's different.

I'm not sure when I actually realised it. Perhaps it was that overcast afternoon of the last rugby match of the season. We were playing Shipham and winning by two clear tries. Dad was on the sidelines ecstatic, shouting wild encouragement, cheering us all on. Mum stood quietly beside him, not waving her arms or anything, just enjoying watching me play.

It was always like that every Saturday afternoon of the season. Always. Then something inside me changed, or perhaps it had been there all along, from the very day I'd been born, only I hadn't noticed it before, not properly anyway.

One thing for sure, nothing would ever be the same again.

I found out afterwards that his name was Gerald. He wore the green and white hooped colours of the Shipham side. We'd played Shipham once before this season, beating them away from home. Gerald hadn't been playing that day. He was new to their side, and smaller, of a slighter frame than the normal rugby player, but, as the team soon found out, he was fast, able to leave everyone clear behind him if he was allowed to break out.

Besides being the smallest on the field, he was also the best looking. Thick black hair cut short, wide blue eyes and a nose as small as a girl's. He was broad-shouldered, but slim and nimble-footed.

"We're going to have to nobble that pretty boy," Steve, my best friend, told me after Gerald had swept Shipham into the lead with a well-run try that had showed up the shakiness of our team's defence, namely myself. I'd never liked playing back, but Tom, our trainer, had told me that I was too heavy and slow to play on the wing.

"You're going to have to scare him, Jumbo," our captain said. "Make it look as if you'll break his bloody neck."

"Don't treat him like china, Jumbo. Hurt him."

The next time Gerald broke free I could sense the rest of my team turning to watch me do my best at pretending to be a wild animal. I brought him to the ground more heavily than usual, fearing for my pride and my team's record – we hadn't lost once at home this season — and let my full weight crash down on his slight frame. I could hear the breath hiss out of his lungs and I moved to get up, planning to rest my boot on his chest as I did so, not kicking him but applying a little warning pressure.

I glanced down at his face. I could see fright tugging at his mouth, and then I noticed the light in his eyes. There was fear there too, but also something else dark in his blue eyes.

Excitement.

He saw me hesitate, my boot poised above his chest, and then he caught my glance, realised I knew, and smiled quickly, curling his bottom lip, as if a secret had passed between us, something slyly slipped from hand to hand.

I wasn't exactly sure what I knew then, but I was scared. It was silly really, since I'd meant to put the frighteners on him. For the rest of the match I couldn't keep my eyes off Gerald, which was just as well as he had two more good chances for tries only I brought him smack down into the muddy pitch each time.

"I think you've got it in for me," he said, in a quiet voice, and I reached out one hand and helped him up off the ground, seeing again the funny light in his eyes and looking away because it worried me.

Then our forwards went to work and scored two tries and the whole of our team pulled together, Dad and Tom cheered from the sidelines and Shipham no longer stood a chance, even with Gerald on their side.

In the second half it was colder and the game grew scrappy. We scored another try and then Shipham seemed to give up and surrender. I tried to catch Gerald's eye once or twice, but he was always far away after that, on the other side of the pitch, yet I had the strange feeling that he knew I was watching him. He kept walking so carefully as if he was on a catwalk like a beauty queen or on stage like an actor taking neat steps across the set. Once when he was ten yards away he turned and looked at me, only this time there was no funny smile on his face because he was staring straight into my eyes.

The blood ran to my face and I felt silly as if some girl had seen me with my flies undone or I'd accidentally trodden on some squashy dog turd. Only it was worse than either of these things because I wasn't unzipped or mucky-footed. I had no reason to be embarrassed, and yet I was. I wiped the sweat off my face with a dirty hand and saw that Gerald was turning away and walking up field. I wanted to follow him, to run up and say "Hi", and see what he said then. I wanted to understand that look in his eyes. I even wanted to touch him, just lightly on the face, to make sure he was real. I'd never felt any of these things before. I think that's why I was so scared. I wasn't *me* any more. I was someone else, and I didn't like that feeling.

I turned then and looked across at Mum standing on the sidelines. She gave me a limp smile, holding her warmth in the way she always did, as though if she let herself go, all the good feelings inside her would run away and leave her with nothing else to give. I smiled back at her, not daring to wave for fear of what the lads would think, and saw her glance up at the grey sky as if she was worried it might rain. Dad, who was counting down the minutes to our victory, checked his watch and called out "Time" to Tom, who was refereeing.

Thankfully Tom nodded his head at my father and took no notice. I sometimes wondered how Mum could stand patiently beside my loud-mouthed father and not run away and bury her head in the ground. The rest of the team liked my Dad. They thought he was a good sport to come along and shout at them whatever the weather. Rain or shine, Dad would always be there, and sometimes he'd drag Mum along too if we were in a cup tie or when it was an occasion like today with the last match of the season.

At one time Dad had felt lost when Easter came and there were no more matches to see on Saturday after-noon, but then he got friendly with Tom, our sports teacher and trainer, and followed him along to athletics fixtures in the summer. Dad would spend evenings reading books on running, hurdling and throwing the javelin, and later, standing beside the quiet-voiced Tom, he would throw in what he called a little helpful advice to particular struggling schoolboys he took a fancy to. Sometimes he used to ask me to come along with him, but I always felt guilty that it wasn't me out there sprinting or jumping for the school, earning colours that could be stitched like medals onto my blazer. But the rugby colours were enough, I thought, and anyway I was too heavy to be a fast runner, too reluctant to put the shot.

Dad always found someone to follow, someone he could pass on his advice to. I used to think he should have had more children, more sons, instead of just me. Some-times I wondered what he'd have been like if he'd had a daughter. And what I'd have been like with a sister. I'd never really had a girl to talk to, no one I could be *feeling* with. It was always the lads in the rugby team and the talk in the showers and the backs of classrooms that should have turned the air blue.

I wondered what Mum would have been like with a daughter or even another son, more children to bring the life out of her, make her smile and tease the way she used to when I was younger. Dad and Mum always seemed afraid to smile at each other, perhaps Mum didn't think it was right to with grown men, and as I'd grown up she'd become like that with me.

Tom blew the final whistle and the match was over. We thumped each other on the backs and half-heartedly cheered the other team. Everyone was covered with dirt and hot and tired. We congratulated one another over and over again, unsure of what else to say. Inside, I think we were all a little sad. Most of the team, like myself, were in the Upper Sixth, and would be leaving school for ever in a few months. We'd never play together as a team again. Before we left the pitch we picked up the grey-haired Tom and hoisted him onto our shoulders, carrying him like some trophy we'd won. He tried to pretend he wasn't pleased or sad, but when I looked hard at him I could see he'd gone all misty-eyed. He kept telling us we were great lads, the best, and he was proud of us all. Not one home match lost all season. It was a school record, he thought. We were great lads. He'd always known we could do it.

Everyone kept shouting, even when we went into the changing-room and threw our captain, Steve, under the cold showers. It was as if we were all afraid to be quiet, worried about thinking how this was our last match together. Dad stood there amongst us all, patting us on our backs and grinning broadly. He brought out cans of beer to celebrate. A surprise, he said, though I'd seen it coming all along. Everyone pulled open cans of beer and drank his health and called him Spectator of the Year, so it all went, I thought, just as he'd planned. I wondered about Mum then, on her way home, putting up her umbrella against the rain that had started to fall, entering her council house alone. She'd put the kettle on, I thought, sit down and drink her cuppa and then set about preparing Saturday tea.

I half wished she'd been there to share in the celebrations, but then I realised all the noise and shouting would have embarrassed her. And then thinking that, I wondered what all the fuss was about. Whether we had really achieved anything? I saw myself standing there on the edge of the crowd with a can of beer in my hand and nothing to say. I felt sweaty and filthy and wanted to soak myself under the hot shower, but it seemed a shame to break up the party.

I'd forgotten all about the Shipham team who'd showered and changed already and were waiting for the coach to arrive and take them home. Forgotten all about Gerald. Someone nudged my arm and I turned.

He looked even less like a rugby player off the field, short, slim, good-looking with his dark hair and neatly arranged features. He glanced at me almost shyly, then met my eyes and smiled as if he was pleased and uncertain at the same time. Then he handed me a piece of paper and I took it and shoved it in a pocket of my jeans which were hanging from a peg next to me.

I wanted him to say something, to explain his funny smile to me, explain why he bothered me so much, but he shrugged as if he thought I already understood.

"Perhaps you'll call then," he said, softly.

I nodded automatically, not thinking about what I was doing, and then one of his team mates called out to him. He turned back to me quickly and this time his funny smile had been wiped away. I could see the anxiety in his eyes, could tell that he was scared, as if he was suddenly aware of my ignorance, afraid I would misunderstand.

"See you," he said, but I could read the tremor behind the nonchalance, and then he walked away, out of the changing-rooms with his friends and onto the coach. As he went away I realised that his sports teacher was staring at me. It was like I'd done something wrong, only there didn't seem any harm in a useless piece of paper.

The Shipham sports teacher said goodbye to Tom and wished us all the best and then he left us for the coach. For some reason I felt relieved when I heard the rumble of the coach pulling away. It was as if I was free, off the hook. I turned round, taking a swig of the canned beer, and joined in with the rest of the team in a rowdy chorus of "For He's a Jolly Good Fellow".

We picked Tom up and paraded him round the changing-room, nearly knocking his head off on the low ceiling. Then, in case he misinterpreted our actions as affectionate, we threatened to throw him in the cold showers, clothes and all. Tom protested that he was an old man with a weak heart, but we knew he was only forty-one and threw him in, rewarded by the stream of abuse he spluttered at us all.

We stripped off our kit, peeling off shorts, shirts, jock-straps and socks, and leaving them in untidy heaps we raced for the faucets that for some reason gave out the hottest water. As I soaped myself I looked out through the steam and saw Dad watching us forlornly like a child that had been left behind. I was sorry because I knew that more than anything else he wanted to be naked, splashing and laughing with the rest of us.

He caught my gaze and flinched, shying away from the sympathy in my eyes. Then he turned his back on me and walked away, knowing his part of the game was over.

I closed my eyes, putting my face right up close to the faucet as if the pressure of the hot water would wash all my troubled thoughts away.

"You going out, Martin?" Mum asked.

I was sitting there in the armchair watching some film on television where everyone chased everyone else through the jungle while spiders and snakes regularly fell from trees onto the heroine who screamed convincingly while music from the man-eating savages beat menacingly in the background so that the rugged hero could remain undaunted. I was quite enjoying it really. A good yarn as Dad would say, and I didn't feel like moving.

"Of course he's going out," Dad said loudly, shutting

my mother up. "He'll be out drinking with the lads. Celebrating."

I was meant to meet Steve and Jim in the Roebuck at eight o'clock, only for some reason I didn't want to go. I felt safe at home watching the TV. I knew Dad would go out and have his Saturday night bevy later on and then there would be peace. Perhaps I could even say something to Mum, get her to smile while she did the ironing. It niggled me that Dad left her at home on her own while he boozed with his lads and told tall stories about the gifted soccer players of years ago.

"You don't want to be late," Mum said quietly, "if you're meeting someone."

"I won't be late," I protested.

"Go on, lad, shift it. You're wasting valuable drinking time."

"All right, Dad," I said sharply.

I gave him a quick glance.

He was still handsome in a faded sort of way, but I wondered sometimes why Mum had chosen him all those years ago.

Dad looked at me as if he could read my thoughts and didn't much care for them. Then he stared at his feet as if someone had unfairly clipped him around the ear. Dad regularly stared like that at his feet and it always worked whether it was Mum or me, only today it annoyed me that I felt sorry. I wondered if he'd perfected this trick as a little boy. I said nothing and turned away, only Mum saw the anger bright in my eyes.

In the hallway, Mum pressed three pound notes into my hand and I couldn't help feeling guilty for taking them.

"There you are," she said quietly, and I wanted to pick her up because she was so small and worn out, looking ten years older than she should have done. Instead I put the money into my back pocket and mumbled thanks.

"Your Dad was pleased with you," she whispered, afraid he would hear.

I was silent, not wanting to believe her, even if it was true. Then I saw the anxiety cloud her eyes and was sorry because I didn't know what to say. It was always like this with Mum. Wanting to give, but forever feeling empty-handed.

"You played a good match," she said again. "I was proud."

That shocked me. I stood there as if my insides had turned into stone. I knew the effort those last three words had cost her, but couldn't think of any way of paying her back. Mum hated it when I kissed her, unless it was Christmas or my birthday and even then she seemed to cringe. Once when I was a kid she'd nearly died when I ran up and threw my arms around her in front of Dad. Afterwards, in the kitchen, I heard him ask her if I always behaved like that. He was worried, he said. He didn't want his only son turning into a mamma's boy. Mum never made a noise. Dad's word was law. Ever since I could remember they'd never argued. Dad said his bit and that was that. I used to hate her for not standing up to him, especially when what Dad shouted at her about was me.

I put my coat on in the hall, knowing it would be cold out. Mum watched me and I could tell she was itching to straighten the collar and poke at the buttons. Steve used to say it was true that women only wanted to serve. But I always felt my Mum, as every woman, wanted more than that.

Mum opened the front door for me as if I was royalty on its way out, though I wasn't at all dressed up, just in my jeans and jumper, though the coat was new. Mum must have spent four wage packets on it. The thought of it almost made me feel guilty. For four weeks Mum had sat at a cash desk at the local Co-op just so I'd be warm in winter. But Mum didn't seem to mind. She was pleased she'd got a good buy. It would last for years, Mum said, and I could wear it when I went to college in the autumn. I wondered if that worried her, the prospect of me leaving her alone with him.

"Have a nice time," Mum said as I stepped outside.

"Thanks, Mum."

It was all I was allowed to say and I didn't even try to take her hand and touch her, knowing she would prefer things this way.

Mum didn't say goodbye, but I think then, when I looked at her, that she was proud of me, glad I'd grown up to be such a tall, strong young man. There had been two miscarriages before I'd come along and I was such a big baby I almost killed her. The doctors had warned her against having another child and advised an operation. I never knew whether she'd had it, my Nan would tell me no more, and when I was with Mum I knew it was a thing I couldn't ask. Sex and babies were pretty much taboo in our house.

I stood in the crowded bar of the Roebuck and supped my Guinness. The air was filled with smoke and chatter as everyone, young or old, did their best to enjoy their Saturday night out.

I was tapping my foot in time with an old Beach Boys record and trying to hear what Steve and Jim were yakking about, when I caught Jim's eye and realised that something was up. I turned to Steve and saw that he was too involved with airing his views on the form of Bristol City to see that Jim was upset. I'd always been good at sensing what people felt, but it was a talent — if you could call it that — which I'd never put to much use. No one talked about what they felt at home, and I guessed no one would here in the pub, and so I winked at Jim and hoped that made it all right. Jim winked back, but I could tell his heart wasn't in it. His eyes weren't smiling.

"You two got something going," said Steve, grinning.

"Any time," said Jim, playing up to it. "Shall we go outside and bugger each other on the lawn?"

I never said much when they joked like this, but then no one else minded, because it was all meant to be a bit of a laugh. Tonight though, I looked across and saw Charles perched on his stool in the bar opposite me. I was scared to look right into Charles' eyes, but I could see he was wearing his make-up.

Charles had thick red hair and a beard trimmed very short. His eyes were always lined with black and coloured slightly on the lids with pale purple or blue. Once there had been the vaguest trace of rouge on his cheek. He always gave me the creeps somehow, in his skin-tight black jumper and white jeans. He was in his mid-thirties I suppose, perhaps a little older, and gold bracelets flopped round his thin wrists, matching the thin gold earring in one ear.

Charles wasn't afraid to look at anyone, though I always thought he looked more through you than at you with his questioning green eyes. Everyone was used to him in the Roebuck and left him alone. Only strangers to the pub wanted to pick fights or tumble him out into the street. Occasionally there was a red scratch on his face and once a black eye, though none of us ever said anything. I could tell Steve loathed him, the way he almost bristled if Charles breezed by on his way to the gents leaving a faint trail of scent behind him.

"Bleeding poof," Steve would say angrily and then he'd catch me looking at him and grin at me, his face relaxing. "You don't hate anyone, Jumbo, do you?" he used to say, and the way he said it I wasn't sure if he meant it as a compliment or not. No one in the rugby team wanted to be accused of being soft.

Tonight, looking at Charles and ignoring Jim's crude remark, I felt sorry for the man, and then just at that moment, Charles turned and saw me. Nonchalantly, he blew out the smoke of his cigarette, but I knew his eyes were smiling at me. I turned away, back to Jim and Steve, remembering suddenly the slip of paper in my pocket that Gerald had given me.

"You've been quiet all evening," Steve said.

"I was listening, in a listening mood," I explained.

"We made enough noise and sang enough after the match," Jim said, running a hand through his curly blond hair.

"There'll never be another next year," I said, but Steve cut me short.

"Don't start that, Jumbo. You'll have us all in tears."

"It is ... a shame," Jim said carefully, as if he thought it was wet to say he was sad.

"I know it is," Steve added, and I glanced at him, knowing deep down he was as feeling as anyone else. "It's just talking about it makes it all worse. It's bad enough leaving school."

"I don't know," said Jim. "Seven years is long enough for me."

"I'll be glad to go," I said.

Steve turned to Jim.

"What about Sharon?" he said. "She'll be off to college, won't she?"

The grin left Jim's face and then he tried to force it back, but it wouldn't fit into his sad expression.

"She might be," Jim said.

"Linda told me she was," said Steve.

Linda was Steve's girlfriend, and as much as I liked Steve I sometimes wondered if he was good enough for Linda, whether he'd be gentle enough so she wouldn't be hurt.

Jim took a draught of his pint and I thought it best to change the subject. There'd been rumours that he and Sharon were splitting up. Even though I didn't want to hear it all again I knew there was one thing that would occupy Steve's thoughts and allow Jim some peace.

"We played great this afternoon, didn't we, lads. That try of Gordon's, well ... "

And of course that set Steve off.

It was as I was going out for a pee that I realised Charles was a few steps in front of me making the same journey. For some reason I wanted to turn back. Charles gave me the creeps. He was the only man I knew for sure was queer, and of course there were stories about what Charles did to you if you weren't looking when you bent down. The toilets at the Roebuck were foul-smelling and dimly hit and I didn't fancy coming across Charles lurking in the shadows.

But before we even stepped out of the pub door something happened that scared me far more than anything I'd anticipated.

A tall, pot-bellied man quite deliberately pushed Charles into his friend. Hardly more than a gulp of beer was spilled on the floor, but they were determined to take it out on Charles, who protested to the pot-bellied man's friend, in a quiet voice, that he'd been pushed.

"Who'd touch you, you stinking faggot?" the friend said, flint-eyed.

The pot-bellied man dug Charles in the kidneys and Charles choked a little with the pain. I could see the panic in his made-up eyes, and I felt sick because he was frightened and I couldn't help.

"You should be locked up and castrated." Another thump in the kidneys. The pot-bellied man looked an expert at this kind of thing. Charles grunted and did his best to stand up straight, as if trying to hold onto a last scrap of dignity.

"I'd like to stick you, Charlie," said the flint-eyed man in a hushed voice that chilled me. "Only it wouldn't be fun, oh no, not with steel."

Charles whimpered as the pot-bellied man hit him harder, only a tiny movement, but I could hear the agony in the whine that escaped Charles' trembling lips.

I had the awful feeling that half the people in the pub knew what was going on. I could feel their eyes burning on my back and the tension in the air. Suddenly it had gone all quiet and it seemed as if everyone was holding their breath. But no one raised a finger to help Charles. Not one person.

Then the landlord, who'd been serving in the other bar,

came back and shouted out. Perhaps a barmaid had seen the trouble and called him over.

"You leave that man alone," he yelled, and I, and everyone else in the pub, could tell he meant it. Henry Wilcox was six foot and fourteen stone and no one argued if they wanted to drink there again.

"He ain't a man," the pot-bellied man called back. "He ain't a man at all."

"I said, leave him alone."

"We're only helping him out the door, to the gents." This from the flint-eyed man. Together he and his friend grabbed hold of Charles and bundled him none too gently through the swing door.

Someone laughed. It seemed the cruellest sound I'd ever heard. I took a deep breath and walked forward, pushing my way through the door. Some loud-mouth yelled out to me to watch myself.

As the door swung shut behind me I thought how the cold air outside had never seemed fresher. I wanted to forget what I'd seen inside the pub; it had been cruel, unfair and I would have liked to have kicked the pair of bullies in the teeth. As I walked into the gents Charles gave a little involuntary cry and took three quick steps back against the wall.

No one had ever jumped away from me like that, as if they were sure I was going to hurt them. Something shuddered inside me and for a minute I wondered if all the beer I'd drank was going to come up again. I looked into Charles' face and wished I hadn't. I think I'll remember it for the rest of my life.

I'd never seen a grown man cry before, but the tears were wet on Charles' pale face, and the traces of make-up around his eyes were smudged. He shied away from my glance and I heard him sniffing and wiping his face with his hands. His expression had been a mixture of child and adult that unnerved me. The trim red beard and moustache made him look mature, but his eyes had been the wide, frightened eyes of a child that had been hurt and knew it would be hurt again.

For a moment I wanted to reach out and put my arms around him and tell him it would be all right, but then my own gentleness startled me, and I took a step back. Charles turned at the sound of my footsteps and saw the revulsion in my eyes.

The vulnerable expression on his face withered away and became a smooth mask. I thought that he hated me, knew I hated myself, only I was scared and I didn't want to see him, didn't want to think about him, only wanted to put him clear out of my mind. Then I remembered his frightened eyes and I was sorry inside, only the revulsion remained fixed on my face and I knew I'd need a knife to scrape it off.

"Do you have to stare?" he said, and I knew that he realised I was more frightened of him than he was of me.

"Sorry. I didn't mean ... "

"Of course you didn't," he said bitterly, spitting out the words as if they were tiny stones. "I'm not a peep-show. You don't even have to pay money to look."

"I'm sorry ... " I said again. I seemed to be stuck like a record.

"I don't need your sympathy, or your pity. Spare that for yourself or for them in there." Charles gestured to the bar. "It's them you should be sorry for. They don't even know they're alive."

I stared at him, not understanding what he meant, what he was trying to say.

"They shouldn't have done it," I whispered.

"Oh no," said Charles softly. "They know best, don't they? I should be beaten up or locked away. Like a sick animal. Don't they know ... "

And then he stopped. We both heard the swing of the pub door, and I turned, saw the fear again bright in his eyes. I was shaking too because I knew I couldn't bear to watch them violently beat him up.

But it was Steve.

He took one sharp look at Charles, then glanced at me.

"Are you all right?"

"He hasn't bothered me ... " I began, and then I froze, because it sounded as if I thought the same as all the others, that he was some kind of animal that couldn't be trusted. I wanted to say sorry, or explain, but of course I was worried to with Steve there, frightened of what Steve might think.

Charles blew his nose into his handkerchief and shuffled out, leaving the toilets by the back door which led out into a side-street. I half wanted to follow him, so that we would both understand. But it was too late.

"Are you sure you're okay?"

I made myself grin and laughed nervously, the sound hollow in the air.

"It was nasty ... beating him up like that," I said at last.

"We couldn't see what was going on, not where we were."

"They jabbed him in the kidneys ... experts ... " My voice tremored and I saw Steve glance quickly at me, and I didn't trust myself to say any more. I could tell Steve thought that Charles had received only what he deserved.

"The poor bugger," said Steve, surprising me, and he shook his head and spat on the floor as if trying to get rid of a bad taste.

Then I remembered what Charles had said and I wondered if that was what hurt him most of all, more than all the insults, kicks and funny glances. Pity. Pitied because he was a queer. Pity could take away any dignity or self-respect he had left, and yet I pitied him, couldn't help that quavering feeling inside me. My insides seemed to have turned to water.

I took four urgent strides to a toilet and slammed the door shut, turned and vomited into the pan. It was over so quickly it was as if it hadn't happened. Then I smelled the stink of sick on my own breath and wiped my mouth clean on a sheet of toilet paper.

Steve called out, but I didn't hear what he said. I was too busy with my own thoughts. My head seemed to whirl round like my stomach had, a crazy merry-go-round that wouldn't let me get off until the final churning moment. Then suddenly my head cleared. The sweat was cool on my forehead. Steve banged on the door, but I still didn't reply. There was one thing I knew I had to do. Trembling, I reached into my back pocket, and found my wallet and the slip of paper that Gerald had given me.

Unfolding it I saw there was a telephone number written on one side. I tried not to look at it, scared I would memorise the numbers. I closed my eyes, saw once again his dark hair and the secret look on his face. I thought of Charles, thought of the pain and the pity, and screwed up the piece of paper, threw it in the pan and pulled the chain, hoping it and everything else would be swept away.

Steve banged on the toilet door again.

"Martin!" he shouted. "Martin! Are you all right?"

"Fine," I called back. "Fine."

I unbolted the door and came out, not looking at Steve, and took a few shaky steps to the sink, leant down and splashed handfuls of cold water over my face. But I knew nothing would wash the memory of the evening away, knew inside I'd never forget.

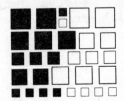

2

Monday began with the postman bringing me the news, in a long brown envelope, that I'd been accepted for a place at Norton Teacher Training College in Hull. I'd be learning to teach P.E.; a B.Ed. in Physical Education. Naturally, Dad was over the moon. I could tell Mum was excited too, but she kept looking at me worriedly, wondering what I thought.

"I might not pass my 'A' levels," I said.

"Course you'll get them, son, if you work for them."

Dad thumped my shoulder and went downstairs whistling, leaving just Mum and me in my bedroom.

"You pleased, love?" Mum said, pretending she was checking the window-ledge for dust.

"I don't know." I laid back in the bed where Dad had surprised me with the news, holding the letter aloft as if he was Neville Chamberlain with the treaty that said war had been averted.

"You must think *something*, Martin," Mum persisted. "Your Dad's pleased for you."

"I know. It's just that I'm not sure ... "

"Not sure what?"

"Do I really want to be a P.E. teacher?" I said, asking the ceiling.

"It's a good job," Mum insisted. "Teaching is. You could do a lot worse."

"Perhaps ... " I could feel myself giving in to the anxious light in her eyes, the lines of worry on her face. We both knew there'd be murder to pay if I turned down the place on the course. And her dear husband and my dear father would be the hatchet man.

"I'd like you to be a teacher," Mum said, quietly, not

looking at me.

And of course, that was the final blow.

"What if I fail my 'A' levels," I said, but I knew I was in shallow water now. In a minute I'd be tugged out onto dry land and that would be that.

"You'll just have to work harder," she said, and gave me a limp smile.

"I haven't the brain for it," I began. "Not for English anyway."

"You're imaginative," Mum said carefully, anxious to say the right word. I thought how she was afraid to say *sensitive.* It was a word Dad didn't like.

"You drew pictures as a child. Lovely pictures. Birds and wild seas and trees. You always could draw."

"It's not the same, drawing and English."

For once Mum was not dissuaded or silenced by the edge in my voice.

"But it shows you could be creative," she protested. "You can think creatively. Isn't that what English is? Creative writing, and you have to think like that to understand it."

"I suppose so," I said, determined not to be convinced.

"Oh, Martin ... " Mum gave me a helpless look and straightened her skirt with her hands. "Your father's breakfast," she said, and then turned and left the room, her footsteps hurried along the landing.

I wanted to call her back, but I knew it was no good. There seemed nothing I could say.

In the mirror in the bathroom I viewed my face critically. I never thought it up to much. My jaw was too heavy and my eyes were too small, not large and set perfectly apart like Gerald's. I splashed water over my face, regretting that thought, and reached for my tube of shaving cream. I still hated shaving, dreaded cutting myself and having spots. I counted my blessings that I'd so far avoided acne.

It was bad enough being so big and tall, I thought. I was never able to merge into the crowd, but strutted around like a self-conscious tower or an ostrich on stilts, only I wasn't able to bury my head in the sand, worse luck. Dad hated it if I stooped. I used to beg Mum to buy me flat shoes, had nightmares that platform heels would return to fashion. Six foot two was conspicuous enough. It was only on the rugby field or playing basketball or in a pub when things grew ugly that my towering height seemed to have a purpose. Then I thought of last night and poor Charles getting quietly beaten up, and I crossed out the last of those advantages. I hadn't lifted a finger to help Charles, and the fact that no one else had either didn't help my conscience, but only made me feel worse.

As I tentatively scraped my bristle with the razor I told myself off for wanting to be a hero. Heroes always ended up getting stabbed or shot, and I wanted to live a bit longer. Then I thought of doing P.E. at college and my future didn't look all that bright. I remembered the phone number I'd flushed down the pub toilet and suddenly I wished it was back in my hand.

I shrugged. I would have been afraid to call Gerald. I would have been at a loss for things to say. But it would have been *someone*. I wanted a someone. Wanted a someone sometime. You could write a song about that, I thought, sing as you played the piano, tinkling the ivories under candlelight. I tried to smile, tried to pretend that it was funny, but I was thinking why I wanted to ring Gerald, asking myself Why? and then running away before I heard the answer.

Mr Murray — we called him Minty — was not too impressed with my essay on E.M. Forster's *A Passage to India*. He said it was *structurally weak*, which I suppose was a clever way of saying that I couldn't put my ideas down on paper in the proper order. "You ought to borrow one of Richard Ward's essays," he told me. I nodded my head and mumbled something, but I knew I wouldn't ask Richard for it. No one wants to look an idiot, do they?

I would have liked to talk to Richard though. He fascinated me with his rambling conversation and the way he used his hands expressively when he talked. He must get his ideas down better on paper than when he's speaking aloud because he was nearly always top of the class. Richard had a place at Sussex University to do English if he achieved the required grades, though I couldn't see anything stopping him, not with all the A-minuses his essays earned.

Of course doing so well at his studies, Richard had the reputation of being a creep, but I liked him because he never seemed to be conceited, never boasted about his grades. In fact I think he would have been happier getting strings of Cs, so that he could have had mainstream anonymity. He hated speaking in class, and I think he rambled because he was so nervous. You could see the reluctance in his face when a teacher asked him a question and of course, being top of the class, he was in danger of being Teacher's Pet.

I wasn't Richard's friend, though if I was to tell the truth, I'd have to say I wanted to be. There was something about him that interested me. Strangely, I sometimes wondered if Richard felt the same. Once, I'd been sitting looking at him, and he'd turned and caught my eye. It was as if we'd spoken then, given some sign that we wanted to be friends. The trouble was Richard seemed to hate sport and he'd been a victim of the bullies and loud-mouths. Unfortunately, some of the loud-mouths were my friends, so the two of us had had little chance to talk to each other.

The English group I was in was a bit of a mixture. Mostly there were girls, some of whom intended to go on to university. Others yearned for nursing, the armed forces or some quiet little office somewhere. Some had stayed on because the job situation was so bad, yet they didn't stand an earthly of passing any of their 'A' levels. These seemed destined to serve in Woolworths or British Home Stores. There were a couple of blokes who never read any of the books and played noughts and crosses or poker at the back of the class. Quite a few more laboured through Forster, Milton and Auden, preparing for jobs in the civil service, an insurance company or one of the banks, and a smaller number, no more than three or four, had hopes for university or a polytechnic. Then there was me.

I read the books, but I only half understood them. I needed to talk about them before anything would get clearer, only there was no one to talk to. I couldn't see Mum or Dad or Steve chatting on Forster's liberal humanist view. I suppose I should have asked questions, but I always got tongue-tied talking in front of the class, and I knew that Minty, as well as everyone else, thought I was pretty thick. After all I played rugby, didn't I, and no one in our rugby team was much of a scholar. In our school all the brainy sportsmen had chosen to play football or do athletics. The rugby team were the Duffers and I was one of them, unable to articulate my ideas, incapable of giving my thoughts expression ... At least I guessed that was what Minty had thought when he'd marked my Forster essay. I suppose he couldn't care about us C-minuses, we made up over half the class.

I sat in my place for a moment after the bell had gone, watching Richard get up from his chair. Suddenly I remembered a week ago. At the blind end of a corridor we'd collided into each other. I'd knocked poor Richard flying. As I'd helped him up I'd taken his hand. It had felt so small in mine. As our eyes met I'd felt him tremble. Startled, I had pulled away, but I'd seen the interest flicker in his eyes. Now, it reminded me of Gerald, only this time as I thought of Richard I was aware of wanting to be close to him, wishing he was my friend.

Almost jealous I saw him leave the classroom talking to a girl. I realised then for myself how attractive he was. Average height, about five eight, but slim with thick blond hair and grey eyes. And there was something about his face, as if just beneath the surface there was a smile, a warm person waiting to be reached. Some of the girls fancied him and he was always surrounded by females. Some boys said he was a bit wet with all those girls round him. I suppose they were jealous really. I hardly talked to any girl except Linda, and that wasn't quite the same as she was Steve's girlfriend and so couldn't really get out of talking to me.

But Linda genuinely liked me, in a different way to how she felt about Steve of course.

Linda laughs confidently rather than giggles and that won me over straight away. Giggling girls irritate me, but that might be because I'm always scared they're giggling about me being so tall and gangly-footed. I have this habit of knocking things over, especially cups of coffee. It's bloody hard not to cry out when you've spilt hot Nescafe down your trousers, but the pained expression in my face has them rolling in the aisles.

I wondered if anyone ever took me seriously. Unfortunately I seemed stuck with the nickname, Jumbo. I was clumsy, I was thick, I played rugby and if I danced with a girl she hobbled off the dance floor with deformed feet after a hearty dose of crushed toes. But Linda had a way of laughing with you, and not at you. She never made me feel stupid, instead her laughter seemed to celebrate my slow-footedness and awkward hands. When I spilled coffee she laughed, but she always fetched a cloth.

"It's about time I found you a girlfriend, Jumbo," Linda would say, and she always did her best to find me one at every dance we went to, only she hadn't been very successful so far. I'd danced with a few girls, even ventured to kiss one or two, but that was that. "I expect you prefer to be a bachelor boy," said Linda, knowing that wasn't true. But then you didn't want to talk about being lonely, did you? Loneliness was a word we never used with each other, though not saying it didn't make the feeling go away.

Sometimes I used to feel my loneliness like an ache

inside, and though I never mentioned it, Linda *knew*. Walking back from parties, or the pub, she used to take my hand and squeeze it for a moment, her other arm around Steve's waist. Other times she used to walk in the middle of us, holding both Steve's and my hands, and I used to kid her that she was mother walking her two little boys.

If I was uncertain about anything I knew I could always turn to her as a friend. Only I never did. You see I didn't want anyone knowing too well what went on inside my head and heart, not even her.

In the sixth form common-room everyone lounged on vandalised foam rubber seats or stood chatting over the loud music, sipping cups of coffee purchased from the vending machine.

I felt lost for a minute, unable to find a face I could talk to, and then I noticed Gordon sitting on his own. I went over and asked him if he was all right. "Surviving," Gordon replied, and then we went through the normal boring duologue that everyone goes through when they're talking for the sake of it to people they only half know and don't really care about.

I suppose that sounds very cynical, but I wasn't usually like that, normally I didn't question anything, was quite content to talk or listen to anyone I knew. My friends thought I was a happy-go-lucky soul, though I had my quiet moments just like anyone else.

But I was changing. That was the sad thing, or was it simply that I was growing up, gaining a better idea of who I was? Gerald had started it off, unsettling me with his nervous smile, and Charles had increased my worries. But it was Richard who disturbed me most.

Again I recalled the look in his eyes when, in helping him off the corridor floor, I'd held his hand. Had he trembled because he was thrilled by my touch? I was abruptly aware of the times we'd looked at each other and, conscious of the other's interest, turned quickly away. I was frightened then.

I was beginning to think about life, question myself and the people around me, and of course that was scary. It was like being given the chance to open the black box you'd wondered about for ages, wanting to know what was inside, only now, when your fingers were on the lid to open it, you had the disquieting feeling that there was something nasty inside, something you didn't want to see. The trouble was, if it had been just a box I was curious about I could have left it well alone, but it was *me* that I was worried about.

There isn't any way you can turn away from the truth inside you, not if you want to be happy. Of course there are thousands of people who don't want to question themselves or see who lies inside. People can lie to themselves, they can pretend that they don't know who they are. Some pretend so well that they can't see the truth inside them, maybe because they're afraid.

But I can't criticise. At that moment, standing there in the common-room, I think I was one of those people trying to pretend that everything was hunky dory. I didn't want to think about what was worrying me. I didn't want to look in that direction. It was as if out of the corner of my eye I could see a stranger standing in the shadows and I was scared to look too closely in case I saw who it was. Worst of all the stranger seemed to have wriggled under my skin, or had grown inside me all my eighteen years, only now for some reason that stranger was not content to stay in the shadows but wanted to step out into the light and be seen.

I was afraid of that stranger. I wanted him to go away, step outside my body and shrivel up. But he stayed inside me, breathing more deeply, becoming more and more alive, and as he grew stronger I was more scared and, like anyone frightened, I wanted to destroy him. But no matter how hard I squeezed the stranger's throat, there was no way I could wring all the life out of him without murdering something that was, for good or bad, a living, breathing part of me.

So I waffled on to Gordon and listened to his tale of drunken adventure, and I wasn't even fully aware that inside of me the stranger was trying to gather his strength, preparing to fight for the life which I, with all my conscious doubts and fears, would do my best to deny.

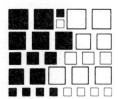

3

There was nothing good on television that evening and Dad, lost without something to do, paced restlessly around the house like a caged tiger. Mum sheltered in the kitchen doing the ironing, and so Dad decided to turn on me.

"I'm pleased about your acceptance from the college," he said, fishing for my reaction.

"Yeah," I said, vaguely, giving my father some more rope to play with.

"You will take it, won't you?" he said, leaning back in the armchair, and there was a slight edge of worry in his voice.

"I'm thinking about it, Dad," I said. I suppose I was playing with him. I thought it would be good to see just who was running my life, him or me.

"What's there to think about?" he argued.

"Whether I want to go, or not," I answered, getting down to brass tacks.

"Of course you want to go." His voice grew louder and more incredulous. "That's what you applied for, isn't it, to go there and study Physical Education."

Dad couldn't see how I could possibly want to turn it down. He'd always sung the praises of the education system and encouraged me to stay in it as long as I could. But then, after working as a porter in a vast office building for twenty years, who could blame him? He hated his job, being bossed about by all the new trainee managers fresh from college. He was determined his son should be on a level with them, only I wasn't sure I wanted to be a college lad.

"You've always taken it for granted I wanted to teach

P.E.," I told him. "You practically filled in the application for me. Well, now I'm thinking about what I want to do."

"You should think what's good for you," Dad warned, nearly losing his temper. "There's millions unemployed, do you want to be on the dole?"

"I could find a job," I said, only I knew I was on weak ground here and Dad knew it too.

"What would you do then?" he challenged.

I pulled at my jumper defensively.

"I could work in a bank."

"What? You a banker?" Dad sneered, treating it like it was the greatest joke on earth. *"You?"*

"And why not?" I said, needled.

"Because you're not the type."

"What type am I, then?"

Dad glanced at me with his bright blue eyes and nudged his nose with his hand. It was the sort of question he wasn't comfortable with.

"You're not a banker. You like fresh air."

I thought he was grabbing at straws.

"It's a good job, banking," I said, sounding as if just this minute I'd sent off applications to Barclays and the Nat West.

"It's a white-collar job," he said uncertainly. "An office job. I want more for you, Martin. I don't want you to be a paper-pusher. You're better than that. You don't want to be a mincing office boy, that thinks he knows it all and arse-licks when he makes a hash of it."

I knew it would come down to this. I suppose I'd wanted him to say it all along and now he had, I hated it. I think he saw the anger in my eyes, because he tried in his own way to put things right.

"You know what I mean," he said, feebly.

"Do I?"

"You're not cut out for an office life," he told me. "You like the outdoors. You'd go mad in an office."

"But what about my brain, Dad, don't you think my

brain deserves something?"

"You can use it teaching. Teaching's not donkey work, is it? As a teacher you would use your brain and be outside with your sport."

This sounded too much like a good argument, so I ignored it and went back to the subject that was niggling me.

"Would you think I was a Wet if I worked in an office?" I said loudly.

"Of course not ... "

"I'd just be a mincing office boy then. You said it."

"You're being silly."

"Am I?" I stared straight at him and I could see something in him back away. I picked up my rifle, metaphorically of course, and advanced. "I'm a man as long as I play rugby. A namby pamby if I work in a bank."

Dad didn't say a word.

"You're such a narrow-minded kid," I burst out, and of course I'd gone too far then.

Dad practically flew out of his seat.

"You've no right to call me that," he shouted. "No right at all. It's you who'd better grow up and learn some manners too. I'm your father ... "

"Worse luck."

There was an awful silence. I don't think either of us knew what to say then. I looked at Dad and he seemed to have grown smaller, shrunk with defeat. I knew I'd hurt him and I wished I hadn't. If Mum had come into the room then and looked at me with her anxious eyes I would have cried. It was awful. All of a sudden I was falling apart.

And then, even then I could only think of Charles, his short red hair and trimmed beard, the worried mouth and in those eyes the fear and the pain which men like my father had put there. I thought of the pot-bellied man and the man with flint eyes and saw my father there too, making fun of the queer, ready to put the boot in, loud and beery-voiced with the others who agreed that animals like that should be locked up. And still Charles' wide green eyes looked at me, alight with pain, the faint traces of mascara smudged on his cheek.

"*Dad ...* "

"You've said enough, haven't you?" Dad stood there in the room like a waxwork, unmoving, and then I think he realised he could come back and hurt me, and he took that opportunity because I'd scared him and he couldn't let that happen again.

"Martin," he said quietly. "You know how your mother is. If she could hear you speak to me like that she'd be so upset."

I couldn't look at him, couldn't argue because I knew it was true. It was then I realised just how strong a weapon truth could be. Dad used it against me now, skilfully cutting me down with the sword he'd found in his hand.

"Think about what your mother would say," he went on, not satisfied with an easy victory. He wanted me chopped up. Even in love, especially in the proud, possessive kind Dad gave to me, there is room for revenge.

"You know how your Mum wants you to go to college. It was your Mum's dream you would teach. Are you going to let her down?"

I was silent as if Dad had cut out my tongue.

"What about your mother?" Dad said, standing over me.

I bowed my head and found a small voice inside me.

"All right," I said. "I'll go."

Dad thumped me on the back as if we were friends again.

"You won't regret it," he said. "You'll have the time of your life."

"What's that?"

It was Mum at the door. Dad and I both started and looked at her as if she was a ghost. I could see her face go all puzzled, sensing something was wrong.

"What was that?" she asked again.

"He's going to college," Dad said, sounding cheerful, but I could tell from his eyes that he felt just a little guilty.

When the face and the voice lie, you should look into the eyes. Dad wasn't so sophisticated a liar to pretend with those. But the words themselves were enough to satisfy Mum. Her whole face lit up, the lines momentarily smoothed away in a smile. She raised one hand to her hair, putting a curl in place as if she was a girl, again aware that she was beautiful. And she had been lovely. I'd seen the old photographs. I never could believe it was her, not until she let herself go like now, when her happiness made even her worn face radiant.

"Martin ... " she said, and it was like I'd given her some kind of precious gift. "I'm so pleased."

I glanced at Dad automatically, saw him staring at his wife, and for a moment something in his face was softer, more gentle than before. Then he spoke and the softness was replaced by the familiar hard lines.

"You'll get your acceptance in the post," he said. "Won't you?"

"First thing tomorrow."

I looked at Mum because the gift, if it was that, was hers. She smiled at me, then glanced away quickly, almost shy.

When she was gone Dad and I didn't look at one another. Neither of us could find anything to say. In the quiet I wanted to tell Dad something, even if it was that I was sorry for what I'd said. But Dad sensed I was about to speak, and didn't trust me. He moved quickly to the TV and turned it on, settling back in his armchair, shutting me out.

"Perhaps we'll try the BBC," he said. "For a change."

But he said the words like it was from a distance. There was nothing personal in his tone. His words were, like so much he said to me, stones in the wall he'd built between us.

Steve always beat me at squash. He was lighter on his feet,

faster around the court, and he had more racket sense. He'd played tennis when he was a kid and the rhythm of racket and ball movement had stayed with him, helping him to put the tiny rubber ball beyond my reach.

"You still snatch the ball," Steve told me as I sweated weary-footed on court. "You should take your time."

"I'm slow to the ball," I said. "That's why I snatch it."

"And bend your knees," Steve advised. "You're not an old man, Jumbo."

I tried not to let it show that I didn't like my nickname. It was Steve who'd started calling me that. I hadn't minded, not at first.

"I'm losing by six games to nil."

"You'll just have to try harder, that's all."

So I did try. For a while I led by seven points to two, but then Steve, scared I might actually steal a game off him, made an extra effort, coming home to win by ten points to eight.

"You see what you can do if you try," Steve said.

"I still lost," I said, disappointed.

"But only just."

"Next time," I warned, and Steve grinned, confident in his supremacy. I was irritated suddenly. Tired of being the Loser or the Goon. As usual, when I was annoyed or hurt, I went very quiet.

Steve won the next game by nine points to two, and we didn't say one word to each other the whole time we played.

"Eight games to nil," said Steve, pocketing the ball. "Shall we call it a day?"

"Yeah." I picked up my wallet which was kept safe with my watch in one corner and left the court for the changing-room, annoyed with myself for being annoyed and in a thoroughly bad mood.

Steve followed, aware something was wrong, uncertain of what to say. Normally he played safe and ignored my moods, knowing sooner or later they'd go away.

We peeled off our clothes, wet with sweat, in silence.

For some reason I wouldn't look at Steve white and naked beside me. I was afraid to stare. Steve still regarded me uncertainly, aware only that my mood hadn't passed.

Two of the three showers were occupied by two round-bellied men in their forties who'd just galloped round the court in order to keep their arteries free from fat.

"C'mon," said Steve. "We'll share it."

It was something we'd done countless times before. But I stood there reluctant, and my wariness shocked me. Since my first year at school I'd shared showers with a host of other naked boys, bumping and knocking into each other, and yet all of a sudden I felt inhibited by my and Steve's nakedness. I was scared. I suddenly knew for certain that I just didn't want to stand so close to Steve's smooth, well-muscled body.

Steve glanced at me, thinking I was being a bad sport and brooding about my defeats.

"Come on, Jumbo," he said. "Room for two."

Gingerly, as if I was walking on sharp nails, I stepped into the shower. I was intensely aware of his body, the shape of his back and the curves of his thighs. My excitement, rising like desire, panicked me and I turned my back on him. My hand grazed against his leg and I jumped. Steve carried on soaping himself unmoved and I closed my eyes and just tried to concentrate on the sensation of the hot water pattering over my body. Steve slapped my bottom and asked me to move over so he could rinse the shampoo out of his hair. Again the touch of his hand startled me. I couldn't help remembering how a few years ago we had come back late from training and found we had the showers to ourselves. Fascinated by the developments in our bodies we had touched each other, excited by our juvenile erections, shattered by the pleasure we gained from shedding our sperm on the shower-room floor. It was the kind of fooling around kids did, there was nothing in it, only it frightened me remembering now when our adult bodies were so close together that they almost touched.

Unaware of my thoughts, Steve stepped out of the shower and shook himself like a dog. He handed me his shampoo. We shared things like that, it was easier in the long run.

I lathered my hair and then rinsed the soap away, keeping the foam out of my eyes. I was so occupied in trying to stop thinking about anything that I didn't hear Steve call out to me.

"Going to be there all day?" he said again.

I turned away, wanting to stay under the hot water for hours. But there were other people waiting to shower and so I stepped out, again inhibited by Steve's innocent glance.

He threw my towel at me and then fiercely seized it and rubbed my shoulders dry. It was the nearest he could get to saying he was sorry about what was bothering me, reassuring me and reminding me I was his friend.

"Now cheer up," he said, draping the towel over my head.

I didn't apologise for my mood. I couldn't explain my feelings, not even to myself, not properly. Had I been excited by the closeness of a naked man? I didn't want to think about it, but I was aware of Steve perturbed by my awkward silence. I wanted to say sorry, but I knew Steve would think that was soft. So I flicked my towel at him, and watched him grin at the stinging pain.

"You're a good sport, Jumbo," he said. "Though you have to be, don't you, playing with me."

"Until the next time," I told him. "Just you wait and see."

"Time for a drink?"

"Of course," I said. "The Albert?"

"Fine." Steve stepped into his purple underpants and reached for his shirt. "Last day of term tomorrow," he said.

"Shame."

"I thought you'd miss school," said Steve, suprised.

"Not likely. I want to get away," I told him, thinking

that what I said was true. It startled me because I never used to mind school before, preferring it to home and the silent battles with Mum and Dad.

"Going to the dance?" Steve dried his feet and reached for his socks.

"I expect so."

"I'll pick you up at eight," Steve said. "I can borrow Dad's car."

"What about Linda?" I asked him, and he was irritated by the concerned expression on my face.

"She can get there under her own steam," he said, shortly.

"But there's room for four in your car."

"That's right." Steve slipped his feet into his training shoes. "Gordon and Jim are coming too. We'll pop in at the Roebuck first, before the dance."

I looked at him, quiet for a moment.

"Lads' night out," he told me. "Next term with the exams it won't be the same, will it?"

"It's a bit early to start celebrating leaving ... "

Steve interrupted me.

"I'll see Linda at the dance, won't I?" he said quietly. "So there's no need to play Mother Goose. I've told her what I'm doing."

I buttoned up my shirt.

"Eight then?" I said.

Steve nodded, borrowed my comb from my trouser pocket and made himself tidy at the mirror. As I looked at him, dressed and distant again, the feelings that had risen inside me seemed foolish and unreal. I ignored the call of my worries and pretended I couldn't feel the touch of the stranger inside.

I don't think any of us liked dancing much, so we lingered in the Roebuck until it was nearly ten o'clock, supping deeply on our Dutch courage. Naturally we all danced better with a few pints inside us and, light-headed with beer, no one was so worried about asking a girl to dance and having an experimental grope when the lights were low.

Gordon claimed to have wriggled three fingers down Nina Spilburn's knickers at the Christmas dance, but the rest of us didn't think much of that story and even less of Nina Spilburn come to that. Still beggars couldn't be choosers and Gordon, with his watery eyes and purple acne, was definitely in the beggar category. Of course his case wasn't helped by his insistent whispered demands that the girl he danced with, even if she was a perfect stranger, should straight away go outside and spread her legs for him. Subtlety was not one of Gordon's strong points and though we chatted, I didn't like the poor guy much.

Tonight Gordon insisted on bragging about his wicked intentions, and he took out a pack of contraceptives to convince us he meant business. When he opened his mouth to explain to us in detail another sexual ambition, my temper suddenly flew out of the window.

"Put a sock in it, Gordon," I said sharply, and they all started at me suprised. Normally I was the last to stick my oar in at anything.

"I was only ... "

"Shut up." This time from Steve. "We've heard it all before."

"I really am going to ... "

"Gordon, for Christ's sake."

Again they stared at my raised voice, only this time Gordon did shut up. I'm normally a very placid guy, but when I lose my temper the windows sometimes rattle. I'd broken Stuart Hill's nose in the fourth year at school. His blazer had been covered with streams of blood that would never wash out. Everyone at school remembers things like that for years. At the time neither the headmaster nor Stuart Hill and his parents were very pleased with me. My own mother was shocked but my father, I'm sure, celebrated the event in secret.

"Take it easy," Steve cautioned softly as we all trooped

out to the car. I wondered if he was remembering poor crying Stuart Hill.

The music was loud even in the crowded bar. Two steps below, the dim-lit dance floor was filled with shadowy figures all trying to boogie on down as impressively and sexily as possible. The air was hot and filled with expectancy. Everyone rushed around like nervous toys that had been wound up too quickly, their scent and aftershave struggling to overpower the smell of their perspiration.

The four of us pushed our way to the bar, ignoring the cries of complaint from those younger and smaller than ourselves. When we were their age the same thing had happened to us. I did less of the pushing than anyone else and it was Gordon whose voice was raised in an order for four pints.

As I waited for the drink to be passed back I turned and saw Richard Ward among the crowd which surged impatiently like an angry sea around the bar. He was dressed in a pale yellow tee-shirt and matching trousers and looked breath-taking. My own throat went dry as I stared at him. His clothes fitted tightly enough for me to be aware of the slim body beneath. I blushed as he caught my eye and smiled uncertainly.

"Hello," he said, and I shied away from his gaze, wondering what he thought of me. The Rugby Duffer.

"Hi," I managed. Then I remembered what Minty had said about reading his essays. Tomorrow was the first day of the Easter holidays. Tonight was my last chance to ask for them. But the words failed me. It was as if I'd forgotten how to speak.

"Crowded, isn't it?" Richard said, and I thought he was just being polite. Then I noticed his mouth open and close, as if he too was struggling to find words. I saw the helpless look in his eyes and realised that he too wanted to talk to me. Then someone at the bar called out to him. He began to move away and then, pausing, he looked back over his shoulder and smiled at me before he was lost from view.

Suddenly I felt the most important thing in the world was to speak to him, but then Steve pushed a brimming pint in my hand and, helpless, I followed him and Gordon through the jostling crowd.

Linda, looking extremely attractive in a dark blue sleeveless shirt and tight-fitting jeans, tried to drag Steve onto the dance floor. When she had failed in that attempt she turned to me.

"Come on, Jumbo," she said, tugging at my hand.

"I can't dance," I protested.

"With me you can," Linda said and smiled, flicking back her long blond hair.

I could see though, from the expression in her eyes, that she was upset about Steve.

"All right." I put my drink down and tried to ignore the jeers.

"Watch out for your feet, Lyn," Gordon called. "It's an elephant you're dancing with."

"Better an elephant than a boozed-up wallflower," Linda countered, turning her back on Gordon and the others. She led me down to the bustling dance floor like she was the sighted leading the blind.

It was a nondescript disco number on the turntable and I did my best to hobble from one foot to another, though I knew, self-consciously, that I looked like a crippled goat with a ruinous case of piles.

"You're doing fine," Linda assured me, reading my thoughts.

But one dance was enough. After the record finished I pushed her gently to the side of the dance floor for a breather and a chat.

It was then I noticed Richard Ward dancing, and noticed was the word. Practically everyone, on and off the dance floor, was gazing at him as he side-stepped, turned, twisted and spun all in perfect time, flexing his body in step with the rhythm of the music. Though it was more than just getting the movements right. He didn't dance like a well-oiled robot who'd been programmed with the correct moves, but like the very alive spirit that had invented them. Unselfconsciously, carelessly even, he used all his body as he danced, turning the stiff gestures of the other slick dancers into flexible, expressive movements that were all his own.

I held my breath. I was shaking because to me he was beautiful, and just minutes ago he had smiled at me.

"That man there wins the prize for being the best," said Linda, half to herself.

I nodded, not really listening. I didn't want to take my eyes off Richard, but when the record finished he moved away, vanishing into the crowd, an uncertain figure again, uncomfortable with the admiration.

I wanted to follow him. Perhaps if we had the chance to be alone to talk ... Then I realised that I wouldn't know what to say. How does a man tell another man he'd fancied him when he'd seen him dance? My desire confused me, kept me silent until Linda took my hand.

I manufactured a smile, tried to mask my feelings.

"Now why couldn't I dance like that?" I said.

"It's natural timing, that's all, Jumbo. Something he has and you haven't."

"Like an instinct?"

"That's right," she said and smiled, and then was serious. "And what about my boyfriend?" she asked.

"He's getting just a wee bit drunk," I said, not meaning to be disloyal, but preparing her for the truth.

"Surprise, surprise."

"Go and ask him to dance," I said, thinking again of Richard, wondering if I'd be able to find him in the crowd again.

"I tried that."

"Try again," I said softly.

Linda gave me a quick sad look.

"Oh, Jumbo ... "

"I can't dance with him for you, can I? I'd be thrown out. And you wouldn't like it either."

"I'd be deadly jealous," she protested. "You're a lovely young man."

"Tell me another ... " I said, my complex about my looks getting the better of me.

"You may not be a matinee idol," Linda said seriously, squeezing my hand, "but you're not ugly either. Distinctly nice to look at I would say."

I kept my silence, my complex not convinced, and then saw a gleam come into Linda's eyes. I could tell what was coming next.

"Now a little bird told me ... " she began.

"A little bird?"

"Yes, it told me, very confidentially of course, that if you asked Margaret Turner to dance the answer just wouldn't be no."

I liked Margaret. She was one of Linda's friends. Red hair cut short and wide green eyes. I had admired her in the past, never with any hope.

"You didn't tell her ... " I said, horrified.

"Of course I didn't," Linda protested, quietly outraged. "You can trust me. I'm discreet. I just found out, to my surprise as much as yours, that the special secret person that she happens to like is little old you."

"But she's too pretty," I said, and Linda rolled her eyes.

"Jumbo," she said. "You are the limit. Perhaps Margaret's blind, perhaps she's mad, but she likes *you*."

I hesitated, trying to take this in.

"Well?" said Linda, curious. "What are you going to do?"

I suddenly became terribly interested in my feet.

"Jumbo ... don't be shy. Just ask her to dance."

"But she's with someone else."

"You'll just have to bide your time and then get in first. It's only Greg she's with, and I've heard it from her own lips that she doesn't think much of him."

"Then why is she dancing with him?"

"He asked her, silly. No girl wants to be a wallflower all her life."

With Margaret Turner soft and scented in my arms my dreams should have come true. But something was missing. First of all, I couldn't believe that she was real, that she was actually doing a slow dance with me, that her thighs brushed mine, that the firm roundness of her breasts were pressed against my chest. We were both nervous and dancing ever so slowly like worn-out metronomes. Even at this restful pace, I had crushed her toes twice and mumbled apologies, though she never complained.

But something wasn't right. It wasn't just my nervousness and the stiffness in my arms and legs, it was something worse, a feeling that frightened me so badly I wanted to push her away before the record finished and find some space of my own.

Quite simply, I didn't want her. I didn't want her in the least. And yet the face of this gentle, attractive girl had filled my thoughts when I'd lain alone at nights. I'd even imagined making love to her as I cried out with the pleasure I'd given myself a little guiltily in my single bed. In the last months if the body I'd envisioned entering had had a face it had been Margaret's. And now this, this *nothing*. I felt betrayed. And worse, I felt lost, left to drift alone and helpless like an empty bottle cast out to sea.

And all the while I danced with her I was thinking of Richard, and my feelings for him when I'd seen him dance. I couldn't help wondering what it would be like dancing with him, the two of us holding each other ...

But that was impossible, something that could never be. Then the closeness of Margaret frightened me, as if she threatened what I truly wanted. When the record finished, I thanked her for the dance in strained, clipped tones and then turned away, trying not to see the hurt and disappointment I'd engraved on her puzzled face.

Outside the Manor dance hall the sound of music was faint, a hum lost in the rush of the wind. I took deep breaths of the cold night air, and looked around for a place where I could be on my own. Turning left I walked down a crazy-paving path, startled by the sound of suppressed laughter, the sight of a busy couple locked together against a wall. I could feel the blood run to my face. I kept my eyes averted and pushed past, walking quickly until I emerged into the green seclusion of a garden. In the summer I supposed parties of people would come out here on the lawn, wandering idly with fragile glasses in their hands.

It was cold out here, peaceful after the noise and bustle inside. The wind lifted a curl of hair from my face and I closed my eyes thinking I could do without people forever. Then I heard the light sound of footsteps and I wanted to run away. I couldn't have faced Linda. She would have looked into my frightened face and taken my hand and asked me, in a gentle way I could not have refused, what I was afraid of.

But no one must know. That was the only thought in my head. I was scared of anyone finding me, frightened that someone might see me for what I really was, perceiving the stranger hidden inside.

I whimpered then like a tiny child. The stranger was too strong now. He was fighting for recognition and I knew then I couldn't pretend any more. I couldn't ...

I looked up at the night sky and the stars spread above and they seemed so far away, twinkling pin-pricks of light certain in their beauty, mocking me. I was about to cry out, when I realised someone was watching me.

Pale in the darkness the figure came towards me. Then I realised who it was.

Richard.

I shivered, remembering again the times we'd watched each other, the few occasions we'd spoken and when, helping him off the corridor floor, I'd held his hand. It was like the different pieces of a jigsaw puzzle coming together, and the vivid image of him dancing had completed the picture. I wanted him. And he was here.

For a long moment he didn't speak, but stayed there looking at me as if he could see right down inside me, as if he could understand.

From his silence I realised he must have been in the garden all along, must have seen me standing there trembling, must have heard the sounds in my throat. For the first time in my life I didn't feel heavy or strong or tall. I felt as vulnerable and fragile as the smallest being, like a tiny creature made of glass so delicate that the sound of laughter would have broken me, sent me splintering apart.

But he didn't laugh, he didn't mock me with sharp questions. He waited in the silence, not moving at all as if on some signal he would dissolve into thin air. And in his quiet my panic disappeared, the beating wings of questions stilled, and in the calm I found my voice.

"I didn't see you."

Richard smiled uncertainly.

"I was over there, behind that tree." He pointed. "See, with the forked branches."

I nodded my head and wondered whether to turn away and go. But I couldn't escape myself by running away. I stood my ground and was suddenly afraid that he would walk away and leave me.

"It was noisy in there, the dance and that."

"Yes, I know," he said, quickly. "I came out here for a breather. It's peaceful somehow ... away from everyone, away from everything almost."

Richard looked at me pointedly, encouraging me to speak. I felt as if he was aware of the stranger inside me, recognising him as a friend. My instinct told me I had only to reach out to feel Richard take my hand, but I could not move. The words were lost in my throat and, rejected by my silence, he turned and began to walk away.

"Richard ... "

He paused in his step and bowed his head.

"Could you stay for a minute. Please."

I think that was the hardest thing I ever said. It hurt me to say those words, to put forward so simple a request. But I didn't want to be alone.

He came back towards me, taking small reluctant steps. I wanted to reach out and touch him, but I didn't dare.

Then, suddenly, perhaps because I was no longer doing what I wanted to do, denying my natural impulse to hold him, a distance came between us. Perhaps a gesture would have explained it all. But I was afraid to reach out and the words inside me were like knotted balls of wool I couldn't untangle, pictures too dark for anyone's eyes.

"I ... "

He waited patiently, silently questioning the fear in my face. He didn't say anything, then turned his face away disappointed, casting a deep shadow across his throat.

I knew then that hard as it had been for me to acknowledge my own feelings for him, it would be harder still to express them.

"I wish ... "

"Yes?"

The gentle way he voiced that one word disarmed me, and I was no longer scared, but anxious he might refuse me.

"Could I see you? Some time, please. In the holidays, maybe?"

He hesitated, and cowardice got the better of me. Watching him dance I'd been aware finally of my desire for him. But it was my secret and, uncertain, I was only sure of safety by deception.

"To read your essays," I said, lying with a half truth. "Minty thought it would be a good idea if I saw them. He told me to ask."

"Of course." The voice was noncommittal.

"Next week? Monday morning?"

"You'll come to my house?"

I looked into his eyes, sensitive to a question behind the question. Was he inviting me to come to him? I nodded, hoping in some way behind the words we understood each other.

"See you then," Richard said, and the warmth in his smile gave me hope.

"See you."

Without glancing back he walked away. I watched the pale figure wander up the path and disappear behind the hedge. Inside me the stranger stepped out into the light. I saw his face and tried to smile, reaching out my hand in uncertain welcome because I was afraid.

4

I was expecting something grand, with lots of windows, a heavy oak door and a neatly kept lawn at the front, complete with rose beds tended by a gardener they employed to come in once or twice a week.

But 17 Winslow Gardens was one of a long street of red-brick terraced houses, each as ordinary as the other, with no garden to speak of at the front and not a gardener in sight. I tried to relax, shrugging my shoulders, and then rang the door-bell. I could see there were enormous green plants in the front room, but apart from these there was no sign of life. Then I heard footsteps along the hall, the sound of the latch.

Richard, in green tee-shirt and tight-fitting blue jeans, glanced at me uncertainly.

"I'm only half-awake," he apologised. "Do come in."

I hesitated because again I wanted to touch him. Avoiding his eyes, I stepped into the hall where there were more plants in pots on tiny tables and on the floor. I noticed tendrils sprouting from a pale blue china bowl suspended from the ceiling. Being so tall I had to duck my head.

"I should have warned you about that," Richard said in a friendly voice. "We're all dwarves in our family. None of us over five eight."

"The Little People," I said, beginning to feel at ease.

"That's right." Richard laughed.

"It must be good to go unnoticed in crowds," I told him. "I always stick out like a sore thumb. I also have big feet which I trip over."

Richard looked at me directly for the first time, his grey eyes questioning gently. I felt he was testing me out. I tried to hold his gaze, but I was the first to turn away. I wondered if he would read my nervousness as a sign of what I felt. How would he react?

I knew I wanted him, but did he want me? When he'd been called away in the bar at the dance I'd felt he had wanted to stay and speak to me. And he had come to me in the garden that evening, I'd seen the warmth in his eyes when we'd agreed on today's meeting. But these were all the smallest signs. Was I reading too much into them? And yet, despite my doubts, a part of me felt almost sure he was interested in me. I shuffled my feet nervously.

Richard didn't seem to mind my quietness.

"They call you Jumbo," he said. "Don't they? Do you mind?"

"No," I lied.

"It would give me a complex," Richard said. "Especially if I was enormously tall and had huge feet." Then he realised what he was saying and laughed nervously. "Sorry. That was tactless."

"I'm used to it," I said.

"I suppose so, being one of the rugby team."

"We're not all loud-mouthed yobs," I said, suddenly, and I could see him go serious at the sharpness in my voice. "Most of us are good blokes."

"I didn't mean it quite how it sounded. Sorry."

I'd never spoken to anyone quite like Richard before. After the Gordons and the Steves he seemed a different kind of creature.

"You'll be apologising all day," I said, and Richard laughed, gently mocking himself.

"I always do that. It's a silly habit. My inferiority complex."

"Well, I've one of those, too," I admitted, taking a pleasure in being open with him. With Steve and Gordon self-doubts and worries were something I had to hide.

"That surprises me," said Richard, turning and looking at me again. "I always thought of you as quite sure of yourself."

"It's an illusion," I said, trying to smile because suddenly I was very nervous.

"Yes," said Richard slowly, "I realised that the other night, at the dance."

I turned round, unsure of what to say and found all the words I'd carefully rehearsed to explain myself had been stolen away.

"Coffee?" Richard said, unperturbed. "The kettle had just boiled when you arrived."

"Please."

I followed him through a room into the small kitchen where they obviously had their meals. As Richard brushed past me in search of a coffee spoon the stranger inside me shivered into life, wanting to touch.

Sensing the emotional change in the room, Richard turned and waited, as if daring me to take off my mask and show him who I really was. The silence drew our unspoken desire closer to the surface. Richard moved nearer and suddenly I was sure he was going to touch me. Instead of anticipation, I felt only fear.

I took two steps away, turning my back on him to look out of the kitchen window onto the small garden. Despite my nerves I knew I wanted him to come and rest his hands on my shoulders.

"Nice garden," I mumbled; and, the silence broken, the surface play with all its empty gestures continued.

"Sugar?" Richard asked, teaspoon poised over the sugar bowl.

"Two," I said. "Please."

He handed me a mug, not looking at my face any more.

"You can go into the front room and sit down," he said, matter-of-factly. "I'll go get the essays you came for."

He said nothing as we drank our coffee. I pretended to look through his essays neatly written on A4 paper. I wasn't taking one word in, but I was afraid to look up. I could sense him moving restlessly in the armchair opposite me.

"You'll bring the essays back, won't you?" he said at last. "I'll want to revise from them this holiday."

"Oh yes," I mumbled. "Of course."

"You could post them if you like," he said, calmly, and I was horrified because it meant I wouldn't see him again for weeks. I was suddenly convinced that I'd imagined everything, that he felt no desire for me at all. Immediately, I wanted to get out of his house.

I stood up quickly, heavy-footed with embarrassment, and knocked over the mug that had been resting at my feet. Coffee soaked into the beige carpet. I think I wanted to die then.

"Shit," I said, always one to choose my words carefully. "I'm sorry."

"Never mind."

Richard rushed into the kitchen to fetch a cloth, and I stared mortified at the dark stain on the carpet as if it was my own blood.

"I'm such a fucking clumsy oaf," I said, my vocabulary falling apart, as he came back into the room.

"It'll come away," Richard said, kneeling and rubbing at the stain with a cloth. "Don't worry."

"I hate being clumsy," I told him all in a rush. "I hate my nickname. I lied about that. Don't call me Jumbo. Please."

"All right," Richard said, persevering with the cloth. "I'll remember that."

I stood there watching him. He was kneeling at my feet. I only had to reach out and I could have stroked his hair. He was smaller and slighter than me. I could have reached down, taken his arms and lifted him up just like that.

"I'd better go," I said, slowly. "Before I ruin anything else."

"The carpet will be fine. Don't worry." He folded the cloth up neatly and without looking at me said, in a voice too loud to be casual, "You don't have to go."

Because it was what I wanted to hear, I panicked. Taking quick steps to the door I left the essays on the chair and stood awkwardly in the hall.

"I'd better go," I said again.

Richard stood up. I couldn't see his face, it was turned away from me. He saw the essays I'd left behind and picked them up, came over and handed them to me.

"Thanks," I said, and took a blind step towards the front door. There was the clinking sound of my head colliding with the china bowl suspended from the hall ceiling.

Richard laughed, and then stopped himself.

"Are you all right?"

The gentleness in his voice made me want to stay, but awkwardness got the better of me.

"I'd better go," I mumbled.

"You've said that three times in the last minute."

His directness gave me courage and, as I turned back and looked at him, I actually said what I wanted to say.

"Would you come out for a drink?"

Richard hesitated and I was sure he'd say no. But he smiled.

"All right."

He seemed to look right inside me. I shivered.

"Thursday, okay?"

"Fine. Where shall we meet?"

"The Weavers. Eight o'clock."

He nodded, still smiling, and I wanted to squeeze his hand. I was suddenly happy. The spilled coffee didn't matter anymore. What counted was seeing Richard again.

"It's Linda," Mum said, handing me the phone and discreetly leaving the room, shutting the door behind her.

"How are you Jumbo?" Linda's voice.

"Fine."

"I didn't see much of you at the dance last week."

"I went for a walk in the garden outside."

"You disappeared suddenly ... Margaret enjoyed her dance."

"Oh."

Linda laughed at what she thought was my shyness.

"Jumbo. Will you come out for a drink Thursday?"

I closed my eyes, tried to make my voice sound casual.

"I can't make it then ... I'm playing squash. With Steve."

There was a long silence and then I realised my mistake.

"But Steve's taking me out for a drink ... " Her voice trailed off, puzzled. "Jumbo ... "

"I must have mixed up the dates," I said hurriedly.

"So you'll come out for a drink then?"

"Um ... well, no, I'm afraid I can't make it."

There was another pause.

"Jumbo, you're being very mysterious."

I laughed nervously, but I didn't say anything.

"So you can't make it," Linda said at last, and I could detect the hurt in her voice at my deception.

"No," I said, guiltiness bringing the blood to my face. "Sorry."

"That's all right. Perhaps I'll see you Friday?"

"Yes, maybe ... I ... " I took a breath. "Bye then, Linda. Thanks for ringing."

I put down the phone before she could say another word. Perspiration glistened wet on my brow. In some curious way I felt I'd committed a crime.

The guilty feeling returned to me a couple of days later when I was in the paperback department of the biggest bookshop in town.

Gingerly I took the book I wanted from the shelf and waited for some secret alarm system to go off, making everyone else in the shop turn and look at me.

It was absurd really. E.M. Forster was regarded as one of the greatest writers of the twentieth century. I was studying him for my 'A' level — and yet, holding the novel he'd written in secret all those years ago, I felt as if I was intending to buy pornography.

The novel I so badly wanted to read was called *Maurice*, the title being the name of the central character who was in love with another man.

I picked up two other Forster novels, *Howards End* and *Where Angels Fear to Tread,* hoping they would serve as camouflage. The sales assistant would just think I was interested in the art of Forster, possibly studying him for a university course. I looked a year or so older than I was. She'd never know.

All the same I was trembling inside when, as casually as I could, I put the three paperbacks face down on the counter, hoping that all she'd look at was the price.

When she'd calmly taken the money, treating me no different from any other customer, and not giving me the slightest suspicious look, I picked up the bag she'd put the books in and left the shop as quickly as I could. When I stood outside, the noise of the town traffic loud in my ears, I couldn't help smiling at myself. It was as if I'd smuggled top secret documents out of a Russian embassy.

There was no reason why I shouldn't read *Maurice,* only I was afraid of what other people might think. I realised then how strong an influence What People Thought was on our lives. Steve was afraid to be gentle with Linda when the lads were around in case they thought he was soft. Dad had used to ice-skate in competitions when he was my age, but he never admitted this to Tom or the sporting lads at school, in case they thought he was a poof.

We shouldn't be afraid of ourselves, I thought. Shouldn't be ashamed of what we are. But then I remembered the stranger inside me, recalled the look in Richard's eyes, imagined us holding each other, and what my parents would think if they knew. I roughly pushed the stranger back into the dark and tried to forget who I was.

At ten past eight on Thursday evening I walked into Cinema One of the Classic to see the latest space adventure. With a large packet of Maltesers in my hand, I settled down in the darkness and tried to black out my thoughts and become absorbed in the spectacular special effects and the familiar rugged profile of Sean Connery, seen this time through a space helmet.

The film might have been exciting, but I couldn't concentrate on it, my eyes continually returning to my wristwatch, the quartz-powered figures glowing luminously in the dark.

It was two minutes past nine. Richard would have been waiting for me in the Weavers for over an hour now. I wondered what he was thinking and feeling, if he was still sitting there in the bar waiting. I hoped he'd gone home, but I couldn't remove from my mind the picture of him sitting alone on a stool in the corner, the hurt in his eyes.

Trying to forget, I turned my attention back to the screen as Sean Connery rejected the pleas of a tearful lover and walked out to do battle.

I sat there until the very last credit had vanished from the screen. Nearly everyone else had filed out already. Taking my time I walked up the red carpeted aisle to the Exit light, ignoring the cry of an aged usherette who urged me to hurry up. "We're not paid to stay here all night," she complained to her assistant.

Walking out into the cold night air, I shoved my hands deep into my pockets. I looked around quickly, worried that I might bump into someone I knew. Crossing a road, I took a turning that led into a winding back-street dimly lit by antiquated street lamps.

Gradually, I slowed my pace, listening intently, relaxing when there were no footsteps, nothing except for the faint murmur of night traffic from the main road behind me.

I turned my face up to the stars, but found no comfort in their brightness. I felt as if they were a thousand glittering eyes intent on me, aware of my betrayal.

I hated myself then. Hated what I was. Hated what I was trying to be. I couldn't destroy the stranger inside me, I could only ignore him, shutting my ears to his pleas for freedom. I tried to pretend that everything was all right, that I could be complete without him. But even in the silence, I could hear the stranger's cries, plaintive like the entreaties of a child shut up in darkness.

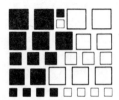

5

Mum always knocked before coming into my bedroom. It would have horrified her to catch me in a state of undress. "You're a young man now, not a boy," she'd said once, dodging my affectionate arms, as if that meant we couldn't touch, even though as a baby she'd hugged me naked in her arms.

"Come in," I called out, pulling back the blankets and trying to sit up.

"I brought you your cup of tea," she said, resting a mug on my bedside table. "Sleep well?"

I nodded, bleary-eyed.

She hesitated at the bedroom door, Dad's mug of tea balanced on her tray.

"Someone rang for you last night. Twice they called."

I was too worried to look in her direction, uncertain what my eyes would betray.

"Richard it was. He wanted you to ring back some time."

"I see."

I swallowed, feeling guilty and ashamed. What I felt for Richard had grown through the way he was attracted to the stranger he alone perceived inside me. There was an openness about his actions, a sense of trust that I'd betrayed in breaking the arrangement I'd made to see him.

"Did you have a nice time last night?" Mum said.

"It was okay," I lied.

Again, I despised myself for being afraid of my feelings for Richard. I wanted to hold his slim dancer's body and be comforted by the gentle person inside.

Mum half smiled at me, lost in my thoughts.

"You youngsters," she said. "Don't know how to enjoy yourselves."

I nodded my head, not really listening. All I could think of was that in Richard I'd found someone who brought alive feelings no girl had ever touched. For the first time I wanted someone, I'd found what I longed for, yet, despite my desire, I was running away.

Linda called unexpectedly and we arranged to meet in the town park. I was dreading meeting her, worried that she'd ask me awkward questions.

The last few days I'd wandered around the house hardly saying a word to anyone. Dad complained that I was in one of my moods. Mum didn't say anything, but I could feel her eyes turned on me anxiously, and sense her unvoiced worries. For once her quiet display of concern irritated me and I wanted to push her away when she was near me. I couldn't bear her silent watching.

In all this time Richard never rang. I told myself that I mustn't see him, that I didn't even want to see him, yet all the while there was the nagging hope inside me that he would call and ask to see me. Every time the telephone rang I started, half-excited, half-afraid. But it was never him.

I returned his essays by post, tearing up the dozen notes I'd written to go with them, telling myself it was better to say nothing, foolish to try and explain.

And then there was Linda.

We walked over the grass where young people played, chasing footballs and each other, laughing and shouting their own silly daring obscenities.

"And *tits* to you Mark Connor," one angry little girl yelled at the top of her voice.

The small boy in question paused speechless, then pedalled furiously away on his miniature bicycle.

"Aren't children lovely?" Linda said.

The sun beamed at us a little uncertainly, promising that summer was on its way. Leaves began to deck the branches of the trees that had for so long been naked.

"Don't you like children?" Linda asked, when I said nothing.

"They're okay," I said, unconvinced.

"But you're going to *teach*." Linda was horrified.

"I know ... "

"Don't you want to go to teacher training college?" The inevitable question.

"I'm not sure." I looked around me vaguely, aware of the feebleness of my ambition. "There isn't much else I want to do instead."

"There's tons you could do." Linda paused in her step to think. "Banking. The civil service."

"Nothing terribly exciting."

"Jumbo ... " she sighed. "What about journalism then, or advertising? You'll have your English 'A' level."

"If I get it," I said, feeling sorry for myself.

"Stop being a misery, Jumbo and think ... "

"I don't want to think."

The words came out with an uncharacteristic sharpness, and Linda stared at me with wide blue eyes.

"Sorry ... " she said.

"No, it's me. I'm in a funny mood, that's all." I looked at the ground, not wanting to say any more.

"I thought you sounded odd the other night," Linda said, quietly. "What's up, Jumbo?"

Of course I couldn't tell her. I couldn't tell anyone. But my secret kept me isolated. I felt then I'd be alone forever, that there'd never be anyone close, never be anyone to care for. Something was wrong inside me. *Wrong.* The word stuck in my mind, though it was foolish. Nothing was wrong with me at all, only I was afraid of what other people would think, how they'd treat me if they knew I wanted Richard, wanted to put my arms around him and hold him close.

I glanced at Linda shyly, wishing there was some way she could know without me telling her, without me having to explain myself. Though why should I have to justify my feelings? Linda didn't have to explain what she felt for Steve. People accepted it, but would they accept what I felt?

Linda reached out and took my hand, her fingers small and fragile in my huge palm.

"If you don't want to go to college," she said softly, "you should tell your parents now. I'm sure they'd understand."

I was disappointed with her for not realising that it was more than the prospect of college that was making me unhappy. I turned my back on her, turned my back on Richard, and took three steps forward.

"Race you to the swings," I said, and began to run.

When I was a little boy I'd seen Craig Thomas, a friend from school, trap his left leg under the roundabout. It had been broken in three places and his shrill screams had filled the park. Even now I can remember the pain bright in his eyes. He was taken to hospital and his leg encased in plaster, but even years afterwards he'd walked with a slight limp.

After the accident I'd never gone on the roundabout again. No one suspected my cowardice because the roundabout was regarded as child's play compared with the big slide and the swings. A boy had broken his neck coming off a swing at full tilt, I was told. And a little girl had bashed her skull falling off the slide. But I never listened. These were only stories and I'd *seen* what had happened at the roundabout. I'd heard young Craig Thomas' screams. So I'd escaped from the horror of the roundabout to the dizzy pleasure of the swing, recklessly leaning back, confusing my senses with the sky rolling above me.

Now, as I reached the swings with Linda behind me, I could hardly believe my eyes. They were so small, so low off the ground. It seemed absurd that I could ever have felt I was flying when I was on them.

Linda saw the sad lines of my face.

"They're so tiny," I said quietly.

"You grew up, Jumbo."

"I'd break it if I sat on it," I said, unable to believe the thinness of the metal chain that suspended the red plastic seat just eighteen inches off the ground.

"We were kids, Jumbo. You were a little boy when you played here. You're eighteen, you're a grown man now."

I was lying on my bed reading when I heard a peremptory knock at the door.

It was Dad. He stood there uncertainly, glancing at his feet, and then forced a smile.

"Reading, are you?"

"Yeah."

"Good book, is it?" He seemed unusually interested, but I stepped unwittingly into the trap.

"Yes," I said, not wanting to explain.

"Is that the book about the queers?"

There was a silence and I felt the blood run to my face. I almost lied, but then I realised he must have known what I was reading.

"I saw it on your bedside table," he explained, and then looked at me nervously as if trying to read my thoughts, but he hadn't the courage to look into my eyes. Perhaps he was afraid of what he'd see there.

"You've been poking about in my room," I said, angrily.

"I was looking for the Castle book on rugby," Dad said, and glanced at the bookshelf where he knew it was standing amongst my school textbooks and paperback fiction.

I knew he was lying, but I didn't want to antagonise him further. I was scared he'd found me out. He was always keen to know about the girls I'd met at dances. I think it worried him that no girlfriend was forthcoming. He'd come into my bedroom like this once before, curious about my sex life.

It had been just after my sixteenth birthday, and I think

he wanted to make sure I knew about the Facts of Life. Sex wasn't easy, he told me in a guiltily whispered voice as if he was afraid Mum would hear. You could make a mess of it the first time round, he'd said, but there was no need to worry. If I ever had any problems he'd give me the benefit of his experience. He'd thumped me on the back. He knew I'd be all right. I was a normal, red-blooded lad, he was sure of that. Why, I'd probably been up to tricks already. I didn't have to tell him, he assured me, disappointed when I said nothing: I was too ashamed of my virginity. The only thing that worried him, Dad had continued, was my getting a girl pregnant. You had to be careful, he said, and he'd put a packet of ten contraceptives down on the bed between us. They were for my own use, he'd told me, grinning like it was a late birthday present.

Later that night, when he'd finally left me alone, I'd opened one of the small foil packets and tried one on. The smell and touch of the lubricated rubber nauseated me slightly. I'd masturbated and then, dizzy with shame, stalked along the landing and flushed the obscene thing down the toilet.

I'd kept the box with the other nine small packets in a bottom drawer under some old jumpers I seldom wore any more. Then one day I noticed that the drawer was slightly open and the jumpers inside were rearranged. I couldn't look Mum in the face at breakfast next morning, though afterwards it occurred to me that Mum never tidied my drawers. She left me to put my own clothes away. It was Dad who'd found the contraceptives, checked up to see how many I'd used.

Two days later I'd smuggled the box out in a Woolworths plastic bag and dumped the whole lot in a litter bin just outside the school gates. I used to wonder what Dad would've thought when he peeped in my drawer again and found them gone, box and all — whether he'd think he'd fathered a sex maniac.

Tonight, Dad didn't ask me why I was so interested in

E.M. Forster's novel, *Maurice*. Instead he glanced again at the bookshelf and the large cardboard envelope balanced on the top of a mini-encyclopaedia.

"You never did put up the calendar," he observed. It was one of those motorcycle ones where women in various states of undress were caught in frozen poses. Steve had given it to me for Christmas.

"I didn't think Mum would like it," I said, telling what was at least half the truth. I realised then that I didn't like it either, but I kept this secret to myself.

"Mum wouldn't mind," said Dad. "It's harmless stuff really." He reached up and took the envelope down, taking out the calendar and sitting on the bed beside me, so that I could see it too. "It's natural young men your age liking this sort of thing." He half-smiled, intent on the glossy pages, the excitement flickering in his eyes. "I'm not too old for it myself."

I didn't say a word, but fixed my eyes on the curvaceous Miss February, not wanting to meet Dad's gaze.

Dad turned over the pages, chuckling.

"The tits on Miss July," he said, and I nodded my head agreeing, embarrassed because my father was trying to show off his sexuality and I didn't want to know. I thought of the little girl in the park who had shouted *tits* to impress, and Dad sounded just the same.

I thought of Mum and Dad in the same double-bed and I felt sick, because as I looked at my father gloating over the soft porn I couldn't believe he loved her, not one bit. He might force his way into her, or she might be willing, but without love the whole sweating, grinding action seemed as obscene as the dripping contraceptive I'd flushed down the toilet all those months ago.

Dad had a last lingering look at Miss December and took a deep breath, then pushed the calendar over to me. I picked it up automatically and stared helplessly at the shiny pages, waiting for him to go away.

A few days later this letter came from Richard.

Dear Martin,

Thank you for returning my essays. I hope they were a help.

I'm still wondering why it was you didn't turn up at 'The Weavers'. I sat waiting there for hours. Why didn't you come? It was your idea that we met up. I was looking forward to seeing you again.

I'm sure these are difficult questions to answer, but I'd like to hear from you sometime. You only have to write, call or come round.

Anyway, hope your holidays going well, revision and all.

Take care of yourself,

Richard

I must have read it through at least twenty times. I couldn't concentrate on doing any revision, and spent the day restlessly glancing at my books and out of the window. My fingers kept wandering back to the letter in front of me. I tried relaxing by playing records or listening to the radio, but it was no good. Nothing gave me comfort except thinking about Richard, forgetting all my fears and surrendering myself up to him and the stranger inside me.

I thought of going round to his home and seeing him, imagining that I would tell him everything I felt, reaching out to hold him, feeling his arms close around me. I wanted to cry because the truth scared me. I wanted to rest in his arms and hear him telling me everything was all right, his fingertips stroking my face, assuring me he understood.

Mum found me in the front room, sitting at the table lost in my thoughts.

I turned and faced her. Her dark eyes widened as she saw the intensity of feeling bright in my eyes. Too late, I tried to hide behind a mask, creasing my face with a nervous smile. The openness of my emotion seemed to appall her and she walked stiffly to the window, playing with the curtains that were already pulled back as far as they could go.

"I'm going to see Nan tonight," she said at last. "Do you want to come?"

I hesitated and her light voice went on, but I could tell she was aware of something, the deliberate effort to sound calm, to keep the anxious, questioning tone out of her voice.

"Dad's staying here," she went on, too quickly. "You can stay with him if you like, you don't have to come ... "

Her voice trailed off and I could sense her spirit quivering like the heart of a small frightened bird. She knew something was wrong, had seen the shadows in my eyes like dark clouds gathering before the storm.

I wanted to show her the letter from Richard, tell her what I felt for him, explain to her as gently and as honestly as possible that I thought I was in love with another man. I didn't want to hurt her. I simply wanted to give her the truth because I loved her and it caused me pain to lie to her, to pretend.

"*Mum* ... " I began, but the strain cracked my voice and I faltered. Though, I think, she had no idea what I was trying to say, she could hear the import of my words in my struggle to speak.

Afraid of what I would say, she cut me short.

"You don't have to come to Nan's," she said, as flatly as she could. "You can stay with Dad if you like."

And then the moment passed, and all the words I so desperately wanted to give her fell apart in my brain like the scattered pieces of an upturned puzzle. I no longer had any hope she'd understand, that my truth could give her anything but pain. For a brief minute I hated her and bitterness twisted my mouth, turned my eyes into dull stones that gave her no hope of affection.

"*Martin* ... "

I recognised the fear in her voice, saw the lines cut sharply into her forehead and my own pain seemed nothing compared to hers. I moved to her, enfolding her in my arms, hugging her close, and for once she did not glance at me reproachfully or pull away. She rested against me, her face pressed against my chest while her fears were translated into conscious thoughts. Suddenly she drew away and looked straight up into my face, gripping my arms.

"You can tell me, Martin," she said, and I shook my head.

"Martin," she said again, "If you're in trouble, we can help ... "

I was silent.

"Is it a girl, Martin?" she said gently, unaware of the hurt she caused me then, her voice framing thoughts that seemed to have been drawn from Dad's head. "Is she ... in trouble, Martin? We understand."

We.

I looked at her and shook my head again, seeing only her and Dad with no room for me as I was inside.

"The police, then ... "

"No, no, Mum. It's nothing like that."

There was a silence and I could see the look of relief in her face, and then her worries returned making her tremble.

"What is it?" she said. "You don't have to go to college if you don't want to. Not just for us. It's *your* life, not ours."

I felt as if she were pushing me even further away, setting me free in a boat of my own, leaving me to drift.

"I'll go to college," I said. "And anyway ... it's not that, not really. It's worries and everything. I have to pass these exams, don't I? They're less than seven weeks away now."

"Oh, Martin." Mum smiled then. "You worry too much. You'll be all right. I know it."

I nodded my head, wanting her to go away, afraid that if she said anything more, we'd be lost to each other for ever. Mum squeezed my hand.

"We'll have a cup of tea," she said, as if that would cure

everything.

"Right."

I forced the word out and turned my back to her, looking out of the window, knowing for certain then that nothing would ever be the same. The house which had been my home for years seemed like a badly made toy of no use to me now, and my mother and father were two ill-matched puppets with foolish eyes and painted smiles, to be left discarded in a box.

And in the glass I seemed to see my own reflection, only it was changed from what it had been before. The awkwardness of my broad shoulders and the stooping nature of my heavy build seemed to drop away and then return, only now in the way I stood, the way I held my head, and most of all in the way I felt deep inside, I knew I was the stranger.

The young man Mum, Dad, Steve, and even Linda saw as Jumbo no longer existed. It was as if I'd shed a skin in order to know myself better, only in the knowledge I'd grown old.

6

Then, what I dreaded most of all happened. I was being a good boy doing some last minute late-night shopping for Mum, wandering along the aisles of Sainsbury's with one of those awful yellow string shopping-bags that mothers sometimes have.

Finally, loaded up with all the yoghurts, bread and sausages I needed, I found myself stuck at the end of a queue for the check-out. I fumbled in my pocket for the shopping list to make sure I'd remembered everything, while the old dear behind me kept banging me in the leg with her basket. I turned and gave her a look and she put the basket down, all apologies. I was wondering about my bruised calves when I turned back and saw who was standing two queues along from me, stacking all his goods onto the black conveyer belt.

Richard.

I felt the blood run to my face. Just like when I'd spilled coffee over his carpet, I wished I could disappear into thin air. I was flooded by feelings that confused me: at the same time, I wanted to reach out and hold him.

But he didn't even see me. It was like one of those nightmares when you press your face against the glass, but no one hears you scream. I could feel the perspiration run down my back.

As he reached into his back pocket for his wallet he turned and saw me. I watched the surprise turn into the warmest smile and he said my name.

And then I did the cruellest thing. I turned my head and ignored him. I could hear the lady on the desk ask twice for his money. I began laying out my yoghurts and cereal to be costed. A mixture of anguish and desire welled within me, but it was the very strength of my feelings that bewildered me and kept me silent.

Keeping my face averted, I heard the clatter of the till and his small voice saying "Thank you". I wanted him to curse me for the selfish shit I was, but he was silent. I kept on stacking my shopping until I was sure he'd gone away.

The lady on the cash desk, oblivious to the confusion inside me, asked me for my money and I handed her two notes and waited for my change. She helped me put the goods away in the yellow string bag and I nodded thank you.

At last, I had to look up to see my way to the exit. I was shaking as I pushed my way through the swing doors, but once on the street I was unable to stop myself looking for him amongst the shopping crowd. He was nowhere to be seen.

After that I had to talk to someone. I'm not sure why I picked on Tom. Perhaps as trainer of the rugby team, he'd always been something of a father figure. We all regarded him as a benign, understanding man, and always listened to whatever he said to us in his quiet, slightly uncertain voice. If any of the team were in trouble we'd turn to him and, even if he could do nothing, he would listen, nodding his head from time to time as if he was taking it all in.

When I'd broken Stuart Hill's nose and Mr and Mrs Hill were outraged, Tom had gone along to the Headmaster and gently explained that I was a passive lad, never one to cause trouble on the rugby field. To be so inflamed to violence, Tom had said, I must have been unduly provoked. I knew this because he'd recited his speech to me in the corridor before going in to see the Head. He'd written it out on paper first, and learned it by heart.

I'd been moved by his efforts, surprised that anyone would go to so much trouble to help me, but when I'd tried to thank him, he'd looked away and patted my shoulder. "Anytime you're in a spot of bother," he said, "just you come to me and we'll sort it out."

And so, years later, I stood outside 116 Breecher's Terrace and tried to summon the courage to walk up the narrow path and rap on the front door. I had no clear idea what I was going to say, but I needed to talk to someone, and I felt sure he'd understand.

When Tom at last opened the door I was shocked to find he was wearing a shabby grey dressing-gown over blue pyjamas. It was just after half-past four in the afternoon and I wondered if he was ill. Then I smelled the alcohol on his breath.

For a moment he looked at me, as if trying to focus his eyes, and then he grinned broadly and stretching out his arm dragged me inside and shut the door.

"Jumbo," he said. "It's you." Then he realised what he was wearing. "I've been ill," he told me, and I was sorry he felt he had to lie. By an armchair in his sitting-room was a half-full bottle of whisky and an empty glass. The television was on so loud that either the people next door were all deaf or they'd given up banging on the wall and had called the police.

Panicked by the noise I turned the television down. I could hardly believe that the unshaven man in front of me was the trim, grey-haired trainer we'd joyfully paraded around the changing-room on the Saturday of the last match of the season. I think he must have read my thoughts because he mumbled again that he was ill and traipsed round me, taking an old newspaper and two empty beer cans off the companion armchair.

"Sit down," he said, avoiding my glance. "Make yourself comfortable."

I settled down, still shaken by what was happening, noticing new signs of decay all the time; the thick grime over what part of the window was showing, the layer of grey dust over the cupboards and the mantelpiece. A glass had rolled under the television and been left there. The room was in a curious half-darkness, though it was still afternoon, because the curtains were only partly open.

The air smelled stale and I wanted to open a window and draw the curtains to let some more light in.

"Would you like something to drink?" Tom said, turning guiltily away from the whisky bottle. "Tea, or anything?"

"Tea would be grand."

I stood up to help him, but he waved me away and shuffled off into the kitchen in his slippers.

It must have been twenty minutes before he returned carrying two mugs of tea and two digestive biscuits on a tin tray. He'd combed his greying hair, washed his face and re-tied the knot on his dressing-gown so it didn't flap open and show his stained pyjamas.

I wanted to cry when I saw him, only I wasn't Jumbo any more, I was someone older, someone more hurt and frightened. I felt that if I started crying I'd never stop, so I silenced the fear and sadness that stretched inside me like the arm of a drowning man. The words inside me slipped away, and were lost in the silent despair that filled the room and the two human vessels crouched there, trying to make conversation.

"Why did you come here?" Tom asked me suddenly, and the vulnerability in his eyes unnerved me. I think he suspected the neighbours, tired of the blaring television of the drunk next door, had somehow contacted me.

"I just called in to see how you were," I said, trying to smile.

There was a silence and then he rested back in his chair, closing his eyes like a worn-out toy, the wheels inside him too rickety to turn any more.

"I don't get many visitors," Tom said, after he'd been quiet for nearly five minutes. "No one calls."

"I came around," I said, unable to think of anything else to give him.

He smiled at me, then shook his head and began to laugh creakily. I was scared he was going to cry. As if he no longer cared what I thought, he moved unsteadily out of his chair and picked up the whisky bottle and refilled the empty glass. He sat down again, drinking a third of the whisky in the tumbler like it was water. He screwed his face up, and again I dreaded tears.

"Know what I did today," he said, in a wavering voice. "Know what I did this last week? Do you?"

I shook my head, not trusting myself to speak.

"I've drank and drank ... They think I'm sick."

"Tom, don't ... "

"You know why?" he said, his voice beginning to crack. "I haven't anything else to do, not anything. I haven't any friends. When school's over I've nothing, nothing to take home with me. No one at home waiting for me. There's the lads in the pub, of course. The Wellsey. I go there regular. Know the barman and the old boys that toddle along there for a pint. We chat about nothing, nothing that's alive and living and breathing. It's what happened in the past, and that's dead isn't it, it doesn't mean a bloody thing does it?"

"You can remember ... " I said stumbling over my words. "You can remember the good times you've had."

"But what's the bloody point? Every year I get to know new boys at the school and every year I see the old boys go, leave me just when you've got them together as a good team, just when there's some feeling there, they go away ... So what's the fucking point? You go away and soon after that I can't remember your faces. I get your names muddled. And you might write, a little letter from the college you're at or about the new job you've started, but that's all. I never see you. You have your own lives to live. I can't share in that. I can't share in anything. There's just the pub and the old men there and I'm one of them, an old windbag with nothing much to talk about. I'm in my forties, but I'm dead. No family. No wife, no children, nothing."

I couldn't say anything then, could only wait for him to stop. But somehow my presence had opened the floodgates to all the thoughts that had been swimming crazily in his head these last lonely days.

"I used to be good with girls," he said. "They used to go for me. In the three years I was at college there were eight girls. Eight. That's all I remember, the sodding number and the odd name. But that's all. No faces, no faces at all. Just a number. Just a good screw. Part of the game you play when you're young and you think you're doing so well. I never married. I had the chance, but I was scared. Women scared me so I screwed them and thought it was all they were good for. They frighten me now. They look inside me and see a shabby old man."

Tom's voice trailed off and he stared at me, and leant forward as if all his words had disappeared into a black silence, and now was the time for his confession.

"I haven't had a woman for five years now. I can't even get excited at the thought. The whisky helps. A little anyway. And there's school. The holidays will be over in ten days time, ten days. I'll have somewhere to go again, people to see. You see there's life there in the school. Not in the staffroom, not in the studies and the books and the classrooms, but in the kids. You see it shining out of their faces and their eyes. The things you kids do. Play around like anything, so loud and so scared and so pleased with yourselves because you know there's life inside you, know you've got it all to do.

"I see them larking about in the changing-rooms, the noise and the scuttling about, ducking the cold showers, trying to avoid the road runs, flicking mud at each other, showing off their new kit. And all the time they sparkle and you see them grow up and change and perhaps some of the sparkle's lost, but then others pick it up, quiet boys you never thought would really shine, but they do and I watch them, I watch them all before they go away."

"We'll keep in touch, Tom. The lads will I'm sure."

Tom nodded his head and then closed his eyes and rested back in his chair.

"You all say that," he said. "Every one of you. But you're all dead. The moment you leave those school gates you're dead to me. You can never go back."

He took a quick breath and then there was silence. For a long time I sat there, stuck in the armchair as if I was under some kind of spell. Then I realised he was asleep.

I picked up the tray with the tea neither of us had touched and went into the kitchen which was in a terrible state. Plates covered with grease stains were heaped in the sink. An open tin of baked beans had been knocked over, spilling its load like vomit over a dirty table-cloth. A piece of toast, with a buttered knife close by, lay on the table as if waiting for the ghost's supper.

I stood there looking around at everything for a long time. Then I pushed the kitchen door to so as not to disturb Tom, and began to clear the table, stacking the plates onto the side ready to be washed. I wrapped everything that needed to be thrown away in the pages of an old *News of the World* and put the whole lot in the dustbin outside the back door. Rolling up my sleeves, I filled a bowl with hot water and soap from the squeegee bottle and began to wash up.

When I arrived home it was just after seven o'clock. The house was quiet and empty. Then I remembered that Mum had gone out to see her younger sister, Sandra. For once she must have persuaded Dad to go with her because there was no sign of anyone about. Slipping off my shoes I padded quietly upstairs to my room.

Halfway up the stairs I thought I could hear something. I listened on the landing, could hear the sound of strained breathing coming from Mum and Dad's bedroom. I was horrified at the thought of discovering my parents making love.

I stumbled quickly into my bedroom. The cardboard envelope that held the girlie calendar was lying empty on my bedside table. I realised what was happening then. Mum was at Sandra's. Dad, thinking he was alone in the house, lay masturbating on his bed, watched over by the glossy, lifeless form of the buxom Miss July.

Something inside me broke then. I caught sight of my

reflection in the wardrobe mirror, my face split by lines of pain, tears seeping into my eyes.

I had to get out.

When I took the glass of whisky from the barman my hand was shaking. I gave him a pound note and waited for my change, trying not to look at anyone. Putting the few coins in my pocket I picked up my drink and glanced over to the other side of the bar.

Sure enough Charles was there, blowing smoke expertly out of his lungs, the cigarette nonchalantly balanced between his fingers. He was wearing a white polo-neck jumper and pale blue slacks. With his wide green eyes, red hair and neat trimmed beard I realised for the first time just how attractive he was.

I couldn't find the courage to go over and speak to him, so I bided my time and waited for the whisky to do its work. After half an hour I bought another drink and then returned to my stool in the corner, my eyes fixed on the archway he would walk through on his way to the gents.

My second glass of whisky was empty before Charles appeared, moving unhurriedly to the swing door, unafraid to look at anyone. I think I realised then why he came here, why he refused to shut himself away and pretend a part of himself didn't exist. It wasn't so much a question of pride, but of self-respect. Charles wasn't ashamed of what he was. He knew he should have as much freedom as anyone else to live his life the way he needed to.

When I stood in the doorway, Charles looked up from washing his hands at the sink and then turned away, but I could tell he recognised me, could see the momentary expression of suprise on his face.

As he moved to step past me I caught his arm, but still the words wouldn't come.

Aware of the confusion in my face, Charles relaxed and took a step back, knowing I didn't intend to hurt him.

"Yes?" he said, emphasising the questioning quality of the word. He smiled at me, creasing his lips in a pleasant, much practised way. The hardness didn't disappear from his eyes.

"Can I talk to you?"

"Talk?" Charles said, as if he doubted I was using the right word for what I meant.

"Yes." I couldn't look at him. "Please."

Charles hesitated.

"No one's said *please* to me for a long time," he told me quietly. "And you want to *talk*?"

"Yes ... I ... " The words trailed away.

In the silence, Charles checked his watch, a neat silver bracelet around his slim wrist.

"I'm meeting someone," he said. "A client. You could hardly call him a friend."

Charles smiled, unable to resist mocking the seriousness in my face. Or was he laughing at himself? The light in his eyes was hard and unforgiving.

"He pays well," Charles added lightly, and I was sure then that for some reason he was deliberately saying the words to hurt himself.

"A man has to do something for a living, doesn't he?" Charles went on, gently. "They sacked me from teaching when they found out I was gay. They were scared I might corrupt horrid little boys." He looked straight into my eyes. "I wouldn't have touched them," he said. "I'm not interested in children."

"I'm sorry ... "

"You said that before."

So he remembered. I glanced quickly at him and wiped my forehead nervously with one hand. I could feel drops of perspiration running down my back.

Charles reached out a hand and lifted up my chin, the questioning light bright in his eyes. I held his gaze, hoping he would draw the truth out of me. Whatever he saw he kept to himself as he walked away. Just before the swing door he turned round, his features arranging themselves on cue in a practised smile.

"Another time, perhaps?" he said lightly, only this time the hardness had vanished from his eyes.

I had to tell someone. Shaking, I picked up the receiver in the public telephone box. The feeling that passers-by could see who I was through the glass frightened me. Though it was late and few people were about, I had a fear of being overheard.

But I had to tell someone. Otherwise I wouldn't exist. Someone had to know me for what I was, who I was. Jumbo was someone from long ago. He was dead. I was pretending to be someone who no longer existed. I couldn't pretend any more. I couldn't face Dad or Mum or Steve until someone knew who I was, someone held the true Martin Conway safe inside them.

There was the click of someone picking up a phone at the other end of the line, the rattle of the coin and the beeping of the pips before I recognised the voice that answered.

"Linda ... "

"Jumbo, it's late. I was on my way to bed ... " Her sleepy voice suddenly stopped short.

"Linda, I must ... "

The words trailed away and I was drowning in my own panic.

"*Linda ...* "

"What is it Jumbo? Now calm down ... "

I could hear the anxiety in her voice, and then she steadied herself.

"Is it Steve?"

I closed my eyes and held my breath and shook my head and then giggled stupidly because of course she couldn't see me.

"Linda ... Linda, it's Richard."

"What's happened to him? Jumbo, what ... ?" The confusion blurred her words.

I struggled to breathe, my fingers clenched so tight

around the receiver I should have broken it.

"Jumbo? What is this?"

"I love him."

There was a silence.

"I love Richard," I said, and then smiling because it was all over, I put the phone down.

7

The gentle breeze blew back Linda's long blond hair and she sighed, a seriousness dimming the laughter in her face.

I sat awkwardly on the park bench and waited for her judgement.

"Are you sure about what you feel?" Linda said, tentatively. "About him?"

I looked across at the young children playing games of their own around the swing and the slide. A young teenage couple sidled by, the boy's arm around the girl's shoulder, her arm looped around his waist. They seemed so close and so content, and I wanted to be like them. I didn't want to be different. I wanted to fit in just like everyone else.

"You could be wrong, Jumbo ... You could be over-reacting or just confused about it all."

I listened to what she said, but didn't reply, drifting up and down among the thoughts sweeping through my mind like restless waves on the shore, rolling in and rushing out with the tide.

Suddenly everything seemed so far away. Uncertain, I was a stumbling figure lost and confused.

"I think I care," I said, heavily, and shuffled my feet. "It's so hard. Sometimes I know it so clearly and at other times it's all blurred and I don't know quite what I feel."

"You don't seem very sure," Linda said, the hope creeping into her voice. "Perhaps you don't love him at all. I don't see how you could really," she went on, not meaning to hurt me, "in so short a time."

"But I wanted to touch him ... " I turned to Linda and she tried not to look away. I was scared I disgusted her, and then I was angry at her, angry at everyone who didn't understand.

"Would you hate it if I was a queer?" I asked her, and saw her shy away from the fierceness in my voice.

"Don't be angry, Jumbo. Please." She reached out and took my hand, squeezing it so tightly that it hurt. "You have to be what you are, Jumbo. I ... I understand that. I just think you should be careful, that's all."

"Careful of what?"

"Of believing you're something you're not." Linda looked away from me, her eyes following the young couple who now, hand in hand, wandered slowly up the slope to the trees on the hill. "It won't be easy if, well ... if you *do* love Richard. How many people are going to understand?"

I remembered the pot-bellied man and his friend with the flint eyes who'd beaten up Charles. I remembered how no one had stood up for him except the barman, and that was only because he didn't want trouble.

"Just think about it, Jumbo," Linda said, worriedly. "You'd never be able to wander through the park like those two without someone giving you a filthy look, or jeering. You couldn't take Richard home to your parents, could you, and say this is my boyfriend."

"They'd have a fit."

I said it smiling, but inside I was thinking of the horror and disgust on Dad's face, the anxiety twisting Mum's mouth, the hurt dark in her eyes.

"But it shouldn't be like that," I burst out, suddenly. "Isn't this a free world?"

"In principle, Jumbo, perhaps. But not in reality." Linda looked at me, sad-faced. "You'd never be able to take his hand or kiss him at a party, never be able to dance with him in front of everyone."

I knew she was right, but I wanted to fight it. I wanted to break down this narrow-minded, crooked system we lived in and build it again along understanding, human lines.

Linda saw the import of what she was saying break over me like a huge black wave crashing down over my shoulders, drowning my spirit.

"You see, Jumbo," she said, patiently, "you could never marry, never have a family, never have a home like anyone else. It might even prevent you getting a job in a school, if you still want to teach."

If.

Doors were closing all around me, leaving me in the dark. Windows were shuttered one by one, like bright eyes struck black and blind.

"I know it's unfair, I know it's prejudiced, I know it's wrong," Linda went on, quietly, "but that's the way it is."

"Then we should change it," I cried out.

Linda rested her hand on my shoulder.

"You can't do that on your own, Jumbo."

"I won't give in," I said, but I knew it was hopeless. Suddenly all my energies and beliefs seemed to sink down within me, and I knew I was again trying to shut the stranger out.

"I can't help what I am," I protested.

"Give yourself a chance, Jumbo," Linda urged, calling the old me back again like a ghost. "It will affect your whole life, the way you can live. You don't know what you are, not for sure."

I shook my head, but Linda took this only as further proof of my confusion.

Forget him," she told me. "Put him out of your mind."

"I can't ... "

"It's best for you, Jumbo. Forget him. Give yourself another chance. Please, Jumbo ... "

I looked at her, panic flaring up in my eyes. Frightened because someone was taking away my name, taking away what I was and leaving me nothing.

"For me, Jumbo," Linda said, squeezing my hand again. "Try for me and Steve. Try for your Mum and Dad, Jumbo. Consider what they'll think."

I saw again the pain on Mum's face, the tremor in her voice, and bowed my head.

"It's just a foolish crush, Jumbo. You'll get over it. Just put it out of your mind and think about other things. Your exams and your future."

I couldn't say anything.

"There's so little time left," she said, deliberately. "You'll be going to college in Hull and Richard in Sussex. That's miles away from one another. You'd best forget it."

There was a long silence. Neither of us spoke, a heavy melancholy settling down on our shoulders.

Like weary spectators we surveyed the ruins in front of us, afraid of what we saw, yet resigned to the ugliness. Perhaps some day we could build the structure again, better than before, and in the meantime, we could only struggle through the wreckage, determined to survive.

I sat down and waited in the changing-rooms. It was unlike Steve to be late. It occurred to me for the first time that Linda could have told Steve about Richard. And he was so disgusted he wasn't going to turn up ...

I was hurt and angry and sweat began to break out all over my body because inside I was so scared. I made myself walk onto the squash court and began warming up the squash ball by hitting fierce forehands against the front wall. I felt better concentrating on doing something with my body, forcing myself to hit the ball with my feet in the correct position, with my body balanced and my racket arm moving smoothly into a perfect swing.

Then I heard the door onto the court open. I knew something was wrong, because of course the normal Steve would have shouted hello from the balcony, letting me know he'd arrived.

Steve stepped round the door awkwardly.

"Hi," he said, nervously, and turned his head away.

I knew then the hurt of being treated like a sick animal, like something that was perverted, that wasn't right. It was as if, overnight, I'd become hideously deformed.

I wanted to tell him that it was he who was wrong for treating me like this, when I was a normal human being, when everything I felt, even my love for Richard, were perfectly natural human feelings.

But Steve couldn't see this.

My hand was trembling so I tightened my grip around the racket.

"Shall we get on with the game, then," Steve said, curtly. "It's what we're here for."

I hit the ball into play, hardly aware of what I was doing. Steve let the ball bounce stupidly at the back of the court.

"We'll spin the racket first, for serve," he said, still not looking at me. "Rough or smooth?"

We played the game in total silence. I don't remember winning a point. Steve never even declared when he'd won a game. I kept watching him, and moving to the side of the court he left free. Normally, we would have laughed at each other, criticised one another's play, revelling in the glory of a winning shot that left the other helpless and sprawling.

When our time was up I left the court, uncaring what stage of the game we'd reached. Stuff it if it was his match point, I thought, anger boiling inside me, a defence against the hurt that otherwise would have overwhelmed me.

Pulling off my clothes quickly, I headed for the only free shower with my soap-box in hand. Steve, naked, covered himself with his towel like an embarrassed schoolboy. I saw him glance at me unhappily, then stare down at his feet.

"There's room for you," I said deliberately, understanding for the first time why Charles used mocking words that could only hurt himself.

Steve shuffled his feet uncomfortably.

"I'll wait," he said, and turned his eyes away to the two

fat businessmen in the other two showers.

Perhaps he was considering warning them that they weren't safe, not with a queer around.

I turned my face up to the fierce gush of hot water, turning my back to Steve, not wanting anyone to see the tears I cried. I didn't wait for Steve to finish changing. I felt sure he was taking his time, waiting for me to go. I felt hot and sick. I wanted to call him a bastard, a fucking bastard that I never ever wanted to see again. I wanted to tell him I pitied him, he had no right, no right ...

Then the tears returned again, and I brushed them quickly from my eyes, the anger and the hatred turning inwards on myself, jagged claws tearing at the stranger's face, only the pain was all mine.

Picking up the squash bag and my racket I walked quickly out, head-down. Steve didn't even say goodbye.

I stood on the kerb of the main road, my hair lifted by the rush of hot air thrown up by a passing lorry. The stench of petrol left my stomach shaking. I watched the litter caught in the eddies of wind settle back in the gutter, waiting for the next vehicle.

I thought how we spent our lives hiding in boxes. Hiding in houses. Hiding in cars. Boxes with windows and doors. Boxes with curtains to shut out inquisitive eyes. The desires that were secret inside them, not to be seen by neighbours. You were safe in your house, secure, filling your hours up with work and wives and children, the other hours stolen by the TV. I thought of Tom hiding away, alone in the box that had become a cage. Tom had no family or friends to feel secure with; when his work was taken away he had nothing to hide in, except his house.

Even Tom would judge me. Every married man and woman would point their fingers. Why wasn't I part of the regular pattern? Every girl and boy holding hands would sneer at me. Every child, every grandmother, every bridegroom, every in-law, every family would mock me, pity me or feel I should be put away.

Houses and cars, boxes for the happy family, assembled on a production line. Everything made regular and set square. Everything that was faulty set aside and remoulded or destroyed. People producing other people who grew up and married and produced more people who married and had children.

I'd never have a wife or a child. I thought of Mum saying I was content as a bachelor, no need to rush into anything, was there? I saw the doubt flicker in her eyes. I thought of Dad saying I knew where my bread was buttered, laying all the big-breasted single girls, and some married ones too no doubt. I saw as the years went by, the disgust sheltered in his eyes.

And if I stayed at home I'd have to lie, have to keep everything secret. Everything, even love, especially love, would be tainted with guilt, twisted with shame. I couldn't even tell my friends, or the people at work. It would all have to be shut away and carefully guarded.

I waited for the next heavy lorry, rolling quickly along the road towards me. The rumble of the engine. The driver perched high in his seat, faceless behind the glass. I only had to take two steps out in front of it, under the dreadful wheels, and it would all be over.

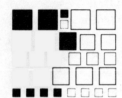

8

Margaret would be here any minute now. I checked my watch and sighed, restless in the armchair.

Dad and Mum were equally nervy, neither of them properly concentrating on reading the newspaper or doing the ironing. I wanted to leave the house as soon as she arrived, but Dad read my thoughts and jumped quickly out of the chair in answer to the sharp rap on the front door.

"Bring her in this time," Dad said, "instead of sneaking away like you usually do."

"We'd like to meet her," Mum said gently, and so I couldn't refuse.

I'd been going out with Margaret for four weeks now, and Mum and Dad were dying to see her, but for some reason I was reluctant for them to meet. It was silly really. Margaret was pretty, polite and quiet-spoken, the kind of girl parents would be happy to see their son dating; but in some way I was ashamed of her. Perhaps because I knew whenever I was with her, that there was someone else I'd rather be talking to. It had always embarrassed and disquieted me having to lie, and I was ashamed of trying to pass off this living falsehood to my parents, and scared that Mum would see the truth.

Mum and Dad couldn't help staring when I brought Margaret in. We were only going to the cinema, but she was dressed up in a close-fitting black jumpsuit with a trim white belt. Her face was immaculately made up and her freshly washed hair shimmering red and gold. Without a doubt Margaret was the most glamorous thing our sitting-room had seen. Perhaps Mum and Dad had imagined me holding hands with a cardboard cut-out or a rubber doll, since both of them seemed shocked when she showed she was *alive* by saying how pleased she was to meet them.

Mum recovered first.

"Margaret, I'm Sheila. It's good to see you too." The two women looked at each other, unsure whether to kiss or shake hands and settling for an uncertain smile.

"And this is Dad," I said.

"Ron's my name, and Ron you can call me," Dad said, and though I thought he sounded awful, he grinned in a pleasant way and I could see Margaret relax. From what I'd told her about Dad, I think she'd been expecting a combination of Jack the Ripper and Attila the Hun.

"Would you like a sherry?" Mum said, and Margaret glanced at me with wide questioning green eyes. I nodded, realising it would be childish now to drag her away, but still feeling the uncertainty waver inside me.

"Right, then," said Dad, helpful for once. "I'll get the glasses."

"Take a seat, Margaret," Mum said thoughtfully. "The brown one in the corner's the most comfortable."

Margaret took the weight off her feet and Mum said something about the exams coming in less than two weeks time. Then Dad breezed in with the sherry poured out into four neat glasses and we all sipped it politely.

I looked around the room and could see the three of them all charmed and pleased with each other. It should have made me happy, seeing my parents so content and so proud, admiring their son's girlfriend, and yet I couldn't help thinking how very different it would have been if it had been Richard there. My parents would have been horrified, but I would have been holding the hand of someone I cared for and desired. I wondered how people could argue about the beauty in truth when it seemed so much easier living a lie.

"They're so nice," Margaret assured me in the car. "Your Mum's sweet, and your Dad's a proper charmer."

I turned away from her excited gaze and said nothing. I was beginning to realise how effective a barrier silence was, though I still felt a stab of pain when I used it to shut Margaret out.

I liked her; she was a cheerful, generous girl and I felt at ease in her company. But something was missing. At first I'd kissed her with dread, afraid she'd feel as if she was made of stone and cold to the touch. But as her arms moved up my back, rested around my neck, I felt a kind of excitement and my hands were curious to explore her. But curiosity and interest didn't seem enough. My desire for her was painted in drab colours without the brightness of a stronger feeling, a warmer passion.

I think she sometimes noticed the chillness about me, and then she'd go very quiet. I would reach for her hand, wanting to explain everything, only when I met her puzzled eyes I knew I was afraid to confide, and took refuge in silence.

"Martin ... you're not listening."

"I was dreaming," I apologised.

Margaret smiled and took my hand and I tried not to draw it away.

"We'll miss the film," I told her, "if we don't hurry."

Letting go of my hand, she reached for the door-latch and then stepped out of the car.

In the cramped space of the cinema I began to sweat slightly. I kept thinking I should be holding Margaret's hand, but for some reason I was nervous of touching her. Perhaps I remembered the night in the cinema when I'd left Richard sitting on his own, waiting for me in the pub.

I sensed Margaret move lower down in her seat and I wondered if this was the time when I should stretch out and touch her tentatively. I wondered if every young man felt like this, whether the whole pattern of romance was merely a numbers game; first her hand, then her thigh, her breast, her neck and finally, in an urgent move towards possession, the place between her legs.

The whole business felt unnatural to me and yet I was curious to know what it would be like to lie inside her. My anxiety turned itself into a nervous excitement and I delighted in the sudden hardness at my groin, thrilled like any other young man at the prospect of conquest, dismissing any respect for her feelings in a desperate, glorifying masculine drive.

I wondered how many men, lost in their vanity and the pride of conquest, were unaware of the woman beneath them, intent only on the pleasure she gave, forgetting to appreciate what they held, concentrating only on making their score. And as they were insensitive to the person in the body beneath them, so perhaps they were ignorant of the spirit that roamed within themselves, blind to who lay inside.

I took Margaret's hand gently and squeezed it, waited for the answering pressure, then turned my face to hers and smiled, wanting only to be her friend.

The film had been boring despite all the million-dollar special effects and the odd shot of gruesome horror. All the characters had been cardboard cut-outs with leaden dialogue. No one seems to make films about people any more, not like the old films. Even if pretty girls went to windows and burst into song and lonely young men tap-danced along dim-lit pathways, it was more human somehow, flickering with life, involving your emotions. I was always riveted to the old films on Sunday afternoons. Judy Garland and Humphrey Bogart are my favourite stars.

Margaret took my hand as I walked quickly back to the car.

"There's no need to hurry, Martin," she said.

I slowed my pace just a little.

"The pubs will be shutting," I explained, not looking at her, thinking uncomfortably about the contraceptives in my back pocket, purchased nervously from the slot machine in a gents toilets three weeks before.

"We could go for a walk," she said, quietly.

"All right."

Reluctantly, I took her hand and we wandered down the road, heading for the darker, narrow streets where we could find the shadows.

That evening Margaret put her tongue nimbly into my mouth when I kissed her. No one had ever kissed me like that before. I started in surprise and she withdrew her tongue quick as that. I was shocked at my excitement and kissed her again, harder this time, and found my senses responding to the more passionate physical contact. I took her hand gently in my own and slid it down nervously to where my erection pressed hard against my fly. This time she started, and I smiled because it was all so ridiculous, playing off each other's nerves. Yet I was anxious to enter her and, in my naivety, my anxiety seemed like passion. I wonder how many others make the same mistake.

"Is there somewhere we can go?" I said, and she looked away from me, knowing what I meant.

I think I was sorry, just for a moment, but then I told myself bitterly that I was soft. Any other man would press for this conquest, priding themselves on notching up another score. I thought of the number of times I'd heard men boasting about how many girls they'd laid. I'd never heard any man bragging about being in love.

Whilst my sexual success with Margaret, despite her hurt, would be admired, my love for Richard would be derided. It made me wonder bitterly just who was perverted, those that used others for sexual gain, or those that genuinely loved.

"Martin ... " Margaret reached for me, but I pulled away and she, in her innocence, misunderstood my anger.

"On Saturday," she said. "My parents are going up to London to stay with friends. They won't be back until Sunday lunch-time."

I turned and kissed her, as if I was grateful, wondering

why I hated myself when a whole host of men would be smiling knowingly, giving me the wink, and even my parents in their own way would be pleased.

"Margaret's a lovely girl," Mum told me as I lay in bed, my face a hard mask of disinterest.

"Isn't she lovely?" Mum persisted, nonplussed by my stony face.

"Yes," I said.

"Very attractive. Lovely red hair. Nice figure and so well-spoken ... " Mum's voice trailed off, as if she'd given up trying to convince me.

"What's she doing when she leaves school?"

"Warwick University. Business studies," I said.

"That's not too far away from Hull, is it?" Mum hesitated, trying to visualise a map of Great Britain.

"Don't ask me," I said. "I failed my Geography 'O' level, remember?"

Mum gave me a concerned glance, and I was sorry for being sarcastic.

"There's nothing the matter, is there?"

I shook my head.

"I expect it's your exams."

I said nothing, closing my eyes, waiting for her to go away. There was silence for a moment and then I heard her footsteps receding along the landing. I was sorry for shutting her out, but angry at her at the same time for making me feel there was only one way to behave. Mum, like everyone else, seemed to believe that all young men should be turned out uniform and regular like tin soldiers. Young men went to bed with girls and if you didn't you were queer, bent, perverted. Didn't anyone realise how the names hurt? Couldn't anyone see that in wanting to love and be loved I was just like any other human being?

It was my last full day at school before we went home to revise for a week before our exams started. It shook me that the familiar corridors and classrooms I'd grown up in over these past seven years were going to be taken from me, and I could never return. Suddenly I didn't want to leave, I wanted to stay and shelter there and never have to go and face the world outside.

I could still feel the child in me, curled up like some baby that I, as everyone, would carry for the rest of my life. Only it would grow more distant in time, fading like the memory of my first teacher's face, or the autumn collage I glued brown and gold leaves to when I was eight years old.

I remembered the games I'd played at school, the songs we'd chanted in the playground, the bully Watson who'd chased me round with the penknife he'd stolen from Woolworths. I remembered hating French last thing on Friday afternoons, breaking Stuart Hill's nose and the time Gordon had burnt his hands playing with chemicals in the back row of the labs. Millicent Winger at thirteen had loved me; her pencilled love letters were in a drawer at home. Kevin Clark had exposed himself in History, and Sydney Weaser had been sick when we'd seen a colour film of a baby being born. In the third and fourth year I'd been captain of the rugby team and had collected a trophy from the Headmaster in Assembly, walking up in front of what seemed like the whole world. I thought of Algebra with Mr Little who'd enjoyed twisting our hair out, Miss Brewer who'd nearly died telling us the Facts of Life and Scottish Mr Bruce who'd taught us Geography, staring at the class imperiously with his one glass eye.

And now it was over.

I was sitting in the back of the class, paying no attention to anything but my own thoughts when the bell rang. Time to go home. A thousand thousand times I'd waited for the bell, whiling my way through Maths, Economics, Physics … until it was ten to four. Now it was the last bell.

Everyone was quiet then, for a brief moment, the excitement coiled inside them.

Mr 'Minty' Murray gravely wished us all luck in our

English 'A' level exam and hoped we would be happy in our future lives. He told us we could come back and see him any time we wanted, but experience must have assured him that none of us would. A whole year of us moving out. Books were closed, desks were tidied and faces would be forgotten. And next year a whole new class, as if we had never been.

I was sad then, and I thought of Tom alone in his house with the whisky and the blaring television. I wanted something to hold onto, something to take with me when I left the school for the last time. After the way I'd ignored Richard, I couldn't expect him to care.

I stayed sitting at my desk, lost to it all, believing everyone had gone, when I looked up and saw Richard standing there by the door waiting for me.

"The last day," he said, and I could barely hear him, his voice seemed to come from a million miles away.

Drifting still with my own thoughts I stared at him and was afraid as he looked right into my own eyes and, it seemed to me, saw everything within.

"I'll be on my way ... " he began, but then he must have seen the beseeching look in my eyes because he stayed there, waiting for me to speak.

"Good luck in the exams," I managed, ashamed of my reticence.

He shrugged and just for a moment I saw the hurt on his face.

"You've been avoiding me."

I couldn't say anything because it was true. Since the night I'd seen him dance I'd known I wanted him. And yet afraid of my feelings I'd run away, run to Margaret and conformity. But as Richard stood there watching me quietly, I was again aware of my desire. I wanted to hold him. But still the words wouldn't come.

"I'm sorry ... It's just that ... it's just ... "

The words trailed into silence, and for the first time we held each other's gaze.

We hadn't spoken for weeks, we hadn't even

acknowledged or come close to one another, yet now, though we were yards apart and without even a single word or gesture, we touched.

It was as if we both could see who lay inside each other, the spirit that folded its soft wings around itself and remained unseen to outsiders, and yet was stirred into life and perceived by those who could *see,* even if they could not articulate or understand.

A wife could submit to her husband's demands, a lover could give way to another's desire, and yet, despite the heat of the embrace, the skin joined to skin by sweat, the two could remain far apart, ignorant of one another.

Aware of each other, Richard and I were startled, lost for words to say, and I was frightened by his closeness, horrified that the weeks I'd been with Margaret hadn't driven him away. I bowed my head and waited, but it must have been five long minutes before I heard him walk away. Only then when it was too late did I raise my head to call him back, but the words died in my throat.

I thought of tomorrow night and Margaret waiting for me in the emptiness of her house where no one would disturb us as we began our play. Something stirred uneasily within me and I turned my eyes to the window and the view of the open sky.

There was a small, narrow room in the changing-rooms that we called the Den. It was filled with gym mats, spare team kit and footballs. Tom used to sit in there sometimes, not minding the musty smell, and drink the tea he boiled in a kettle he had stored down there. It used to puzzle me that someone so kindly as Tom would choose to shelter there rather than mixing in the staff room. But now I think I understood. I'd seen the loneliness behind his easy smile, and curiously I realised it was easier in some ways to tolerate your loneliness on your own, without the superficial conversation of others grating on your senses.

I found Tom down there, but he wasn't alone. A lad of

fourteen called Wilson was with him, sitting cross-legged on the floor at Tom's feet.

I had the awful sense I'd interrupted something. Everything was very quiet and they both looked startled when they saw me standing there. Tom turned his nervous surprise into a quick smile, but the boy was unable to mask an embarrassment and an anger at my intrusion. I wondered whether to make myself scarce, but Tom called out to me as I took a step back.

"Jumbo, come in. Have a tea." Tom busied himself with the kettle, and turned to Wilson. He said something I couldn't hear and then Wilson, not looking at me, pushed his way by and out of the Den slamming the door behind him.

"Promising young chap that," Tom said, as he stirred a tea-bag round and round in the hot water. "Captain of the football team. Bit small for rugby. Shame that, still ..." Tom turned, and smiled at me, but I could see an anxiety huddled in the shadows of his eyes. Perhaps he was remembering the last time we met.

I took my mug of tea and sipped it, feeling awkwardly large for the small room.

"Thanks for clearing up," Tom said, suddenly. "The house was a terrible mess ..."

"It doesn't matter," I told him, not wanting him to worry or feel ashamed.

"I was in a dark mood," Tom said quickly. "I don't normally drink like that. Hardly touch a drop of the stuff."

I wished he hadn't lied, or felt the need to lie. I wished he could have trusted me.

"Wilson often comes here for a chat," he carried on, not looking at me. "Nothing wrong in that, is there? No harm in it at all."

I shook my head agreeing. There'd been stories of Tom staring at the young lads as they showered, but none of the rugby team had ever taken any notice of them. I looked at Tom, watching him blow on his hot tea. I remembered him telling me how deep down women frightened him. I wondered if he too was running away from some part of himself he did not want to think about. Perhaps he too was scared of wanting to love another man. Then I thought how everyone seemed afraid of love, and Tom was just another sad and lonely man, that's all.

"It's our last day," I said, trying to sound bright. "Don't have to come in again, except for the exams. Week after next."

"I know ... " Tom sipped his tea. "Terrible things, exams," he said, then turned to look at me. "You'll be all right though, Jumbo. You've got it up here." He tapped his temples.

I smiled feebly.

"And after that college, isn't it? You're going to be a P.E. teacher. Follow in my footsteps." Tom half-laughed. "Hull, isn't it?"

"That's right."

"You'll have the time of your life. I did when I was at college. The other lads were great. And the girls ... I remember, the time of your life."

"I expect so ... " My voice wavered. All I could hear was Tom telling me he couldn't remember their faces, just the score. Eight.

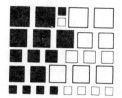

9

It was Saturday night and I badly needed a drink to steady my nerves. Standing in my bedroom, dressed in fresh clothes, I closed my eyes and willed myself to think of Margaret white and naked in front of me. I thought of the narrowness of her fragile shoulders and trim waist, the broadness of her hips. I thought of what it would be like to be inside her, to bury my head between her breasts like a nervous child.

Then someone knocked on the door and I started. Dad came in, gave me a quick glance and I reassured him with a cheap smile.

"Out tonight?" Dad always began with the obvious.

"Yeah."

"Margaret with you?"

"Later on," I explained as casually as I could. "I'm having a drink with the lads first."

"I see."

There was an awkward silence. I checked my hair was tidy in the mirror.

"You don't need anything, do you, for tonight? I could give you something."

"I'm well supplied, thank you," I said, shocked at the smooth confident tones in my voice, though sure enough I did have a pack of three Extra Sensitive Midnite contraceptives in my jacket pocket.

I turned and looked straight at Dad and something in him shuffled away. It was like I could see the lonely man inside him, frustrated with the emptiness he'd created in his own life. Though it wasn't all his own fault. Without an education or any special talent he was stuck in a routine job, delivering messages, sorting post, being ordered about by people half his age with their university degrees. Then I thought of Tom and the shabby, unhappy man that lay inside him, coming out painfully in the solitude of the lonely house. I wondered if Dad appreciated how Mum saved him from himself, sacrificing areas of her life to keep him safe. Yet Mum's sacrifice was freely made. Perhaps that was love?

I nodded to myself, knowing it was love that Mum gave Dad, love that she had given him all these years without any outward show of thanks. I remembered a poem written by Blake, who we'd studied for 'A' level. It said how love should be given unselfishly, and that amid the Hell in our lives, love could create a Heaven, a place of peace. It helped me to appreciate how important love was, and how without it life would be miserable and empty.

But standing there with Dad, I was just like Tom sitting alone in his dark front room with a whisky bottle. I didn't want to think about what I was doing. I wanted to run away.

"Well ... have a good time," Dad said at last, unnerved by my thoughtful silence.

I shrugged away my worries and straightened up to my full height, aware of my broad shoulders and the clothes that hung attractively on me. Before the evening had ended I would have left my nightmare virginity behind and proved to myself, and the rest of the world, that I was a man.

Later, I would hate myself, realise the selfishness of my pride, the foolishness of my desire, and become aware that as a man the only thing I had to show was that I could be a feeling human being with no desire to deliberately hurt others or myself.

"The tits on Nancy Peters," Gordon said, breathlessly. And then he smiled, his flushed face creasing into smug lines. "And I'm in there boys," he assured us. "It's me in there."

"You and whose army?" said Jim.

"Come off it, Gordon. She wouldn't look at you," Steve said, his voice loud with beer. But we were all drinking hard that night.

Steve caught my eye and grinned. Ever since I'd started going out with Margaret our friendship had gone on as before; squash and the odd evening drink. But tonight Gordon irritated me.

"One of your wet dreams, Gordon," I said, being mean, and everyone laughed.

Gordon gave me a sharp glance, his eyes annoyed in his red acned face.

"Got your leg over yet, Jumbo? Maggie's classy, but she's a tight arse."

There was an awkward silence.

"Sure I have," I said, shakily aware that Steve was listening hard.

"About time too," Gordon went on, exploiting my uncertainty. "A virgin like you."

"Now then," said Steve, and rested a hand on my arm as if expecting me to knock Gordon bloody into next week, though nothing was further from my mind.

"At least Martin's got taste," said Jim, helpfully. "He doesn't offer it to anyone."

"Not the tarts you get," Steve added.

Gordon gave us a hard stare as if he hated every one of us.

"Slags or not," he said. "I make them, don't I? That's more than he can say. A white elephant Jumbo is, virgin white if you ask me."

"Well, we're not," said Jim, in a voice that silenced Gordon, and Steve made sure, leaning over and grabbing Gordon's shirt-collar in a pseudo-friendly manner.

"Shut it," Steve said. "Right?"

Gordon looked at me and kept quiet. For an awkward time no one said anything.

I thought what a sham thing friendship could be, and then Steve made it all worse. As we were walking unsteadily back to his car, Steve grabbed my arm, hissing in my ear so that no one could hear.

"Have you laid her?" Steve said, and because I didn't want to see the curiosity gleaming in his eyes I walked off, pulling my arm roughly away.

"Jumbo ... " he called after me, but I pretended not to hear, stuffing my fists deep into my pockets, twisting the lining with my fingers, wishing I could be alone.

"You're both drunk," Linda told us in the bar of the Manor Hall.

"Come on now." Steve pulled clumsily at Linda's hand and for a moment she resisted, turning her face to me so that I could see the flicker of pain in her eyes.

"You're a bully, Steve," I said, but he let go of her arm.

"You hurt me." Linda's lip trembled.

"I was playing, that's all." Steve emptied his pint glass. Linda turned and walked quickly away, disappearing into the crowd of young people.

I moved to follow her, but Steve stopped me.

"Leave her alone, Jumbo."

"She's upset ... " I protested.

"Leave her." Steve wrenched at my arm and I winced with the pain. For a moment we stared at each other like two furious animals, before turning our backs on each other.

Everything was going wrong that evening.

Then Margaret reached out and laid her hand gently on mine. I felt too guilty to smile at her, was afraid to see the worry in her eyes.

"Another pint," I said, to no one in particular.

"Martin ... please."

This time I turned and looked at her, read the anxiety in her face and was ashamed.

"Let's go," I said.

Margaret didn't say a word then. Her face was pale, and the sudden silence about her upset me even more. I could see everything inside her intent on one thought, and then she made her decision and her waxen face came alive again.

As she smiled, I thought how much of a child I was compared to her, playing a game that wasn't right for me, too selfish and too frightened to admit the truth.

As we pushed our way through the press of people, I took her hand and squeezed it tightly. Turning, she smiled at me, but it was an empty smile as if a part of her knew that I was no longer a friend.

Naked, we stared at one another uncertainly like strangers. Our clothes seemed the only thing familiar to us, the signs by which we'd known and recognised each other, and these lay discarded on the bedroom floor.

I turned the bedroom light off, afraid to see her. Perhaps it was someone else pale across the other side of the room. She came towards me. The touch of another's skin was a sensation novel enough to excite me, and I was aware of the hardness I pressed against her belly.

"Have you done this before?" I whispered.

Margaret didn't answer, but I could feel her head nodding against my shoulder.

"I ... I haven't," I said, and felt a little better, glad I'd voiced a part of the truth.

She kissed me very gently and slid her hands down my side and up my back. I copied her, moving my hands nervously over her smooth body, feeling the roundness of her breasts, the hard points of her nipples and the soft flesh of her thighs, the thick curls of hair between her legs. Then she moved away and I heard her lie down on the bed, waiting for me.

I cried out when I entered her, and then forgot the helpfulness of her guiding hands, the accommodating movements she'd made, and it was almost as if quite suddenly she didn't exist.

Awkwardly at first I moved within her, concentrating on perfecting the rhythm of the thrusts of my body, forgetting everything but the hard column of flesh inside her, protected by the foul rubber contraceptive. I heard my breaths quickening, the rasping sound of air in my lungs and closed my eyes to everything else, thinking only of the pleasure and pumping, pumping like I had all those nights on my own. Barely aware of the person beneath me I kept on pumping, pumping, breathing harder now, feeling so good I couldn't keep a steady rhythm. Jerking harder and harder, mild spasms of pleasure choked me, until at the last I cried out like someone scared of being alone.

I flushed the dripping contraceptive down the toilet, thinking how I'd done exactly the same thing months before after I'd masturbated using one of the contraceptives that Dad had given me. The horrible thing was, now it was over, I felt no different from before. Any pride and pleasure had evaporated. I stared down into the water in the toilet pan and felt nothing except a reluctance to return to the stranger I'd left worn and used in her own bed.

I told myself I was a man now, that Steve and Dad and Tom and everyone else would be pleased. I'd imagined that afterwards I'd feel as strong and successful as a giant, but as I looked down into the water it seemed to me I could only see the shaky reflection of a shabby little man who had nothing to hold.

I was glad of the darkness in her room, afraid to look at her lying in the bed, propped up on one elbow. I stumbled around trying to find my clothes in the muddle of garments on the floor.

"Aren't you going to stay?" she said at last, and I wondered if she was going to cry.

"Mum and Dad," I explained. "I have to go home."

"Martin ... "

"They expect me back." Anxiety made my voice loud and Margaret rolled over, her back towards me.

I wanted to reach out and comfort her, but I was scared she'd seize me tightly in her arms and refuse to let me go. I felt better not seeing her face. I tried to tell myself that she was all right, that I wasn't doing anything wrong. I found my socks and slipped them on quickly.

"It's always like this," Margaret said in a very quiet creaky voice that made me panic. "They always go away. Won't you stay?"

The pleading tones of her voice reached deep inside me, caused me pain, but increased my fear.

"Please ... Martin, please."

I backed away from the crying figure in the bed.

"I can't, I've got to go," I protested, and finding my shoes, I hurried to the door.

The muffled crying stopped and I hesitated, wishing I wanted to go back and hold her, but the silence accused me of murder, and the very last thing I felt like doing was touching the figure on the bed, a hopeless stranger I'd used but had no time for.

The bedroom door scraped open and I stumbled quickly along the landing, and down the stairs, listening anxiously for the sound of movement, but all was quiet. I turned on the hall light, checked I had everything and retied my shoelaces. I opened the hall cupboard where I remembered Margaret had carefully hung my coat. I realised that even then she'd been hoping I'd stay with her until morning.

I sat at the bottom of the stairs for a long time, waiting until I heard the soft sound of footsteps behind me. I looked up and saw she was wearing a huge, shapeless dressing-gown. It made me smile because it was much too big for her.

"Martin ... "

"Your dressing-gown."

She smiled thinly, trying not to be anxious.

"It's Dad's," she said, quietly, and then her voice trailed off.

"I can't stay," I whispered, and then I reached out and very gently touched the side of her face with my fingers.

She put her arms around me holding me very tight, and I buried the desire to pull away. At last, she relaxed her embrace, and very slowly, I took her hands and rested them at her side and she made no sound.

I turned to the front door, reaching for the unfamiliar latch. Eventually the door came open.

"Thanks," she said, and I flinched, turning away from her.

"For what," I croaked. "Thanks for what?"

Margaret stared at me, puzzled, trying to see what I felt inside.

"At least you stayed a while," she said, softly. "You waited on the stairs. That's more than the others ... "

I put my hand up to stop her speaking, unable to bear the gratefulness in her voice.

"I'm sorry," I said, and pulling the door wide open I stepped outside, shutting the door behind me.

As I walked down the path I could hear the sound of the door opening again, and I knew Margaret was silently watching me go.

After all the hours and hours of poring over my files of notes it was a relief to be on the squash court, not thinking about anything except hitting the ball as smoothly as I could, making it as difficult as possible for Steve to retrieve.

In the changing-rooms he told me my game had improved, and I smiled, not feeling the need to point out that I'd actually won three games off him.

We showered in separate cubicles and then sat side by side on the benches, drying ourselves with thick towels.

"Margaret's helping your game," said Steve, giving me a quick side-glance.

I nodded slightly and started drying my hair. It occurred to me that Margaret might have confided to Linda, and that Linda might have passed on the word to Steve. I supposed all three of them would be pleased now I'd proven I was a normal heterosexual male.

Someone inside me wanted to laugh at them. I remembered Charles talking about the misguided people in the bar of the Roebuck. *They don't even know they're alive.* Then I thought of the pain in Charles' eyes, and the violent contempt of the pot-bellied man and his flint-eyed friend, and nothing seemed funny at all.

"Seen Margaret since Saturday, Jumbo?" Steve hesitated over the word Saturday and smiled slightly.

I wondered if he wanted me to draw pictures, to say exactly what I'd done and what it felt like.

"Too busy revising," I said stiffly.

Steve smiled knowingly, nodding his head like one of those puppets you see in the backs of cars.

"That's right, Jumbo. You keep your distance. That's how to handle girls. You can't be soft with them, can't let them get too close."

I reached for my shirt and said nothing. There was no anger inside me, no resentment, just a dull ache, as if I'd opened the lid on myself and, peering inside, had become aware of the cold, empty darkness there. I wondered if Steve and the others went around like this all the time, hollow shells with no wash of feeling, their lives dictated by appearance, what people thought of them, how they felt they should behave, being what other people expected them to be.

"You've got to let women know who's in control ... "

"Isn't that unfeeling?"

Steve looked at me, startled like a young boy.

"It's not like friendship, is it?" he said quickly. "I mean, you don't sleep with a friend."

But you should, I wanted to say. If men were friends with women the war between the sexes would be over.

I didn't say anything, just buckled the belt of my jeans and reached down for my shoes.

"Sex is great, isn't it?" Steve said, turning his face into a wide monkey grin. "Nothing beats a good lay."

"Yeah ... "

The word came out easily enough and I saw Steve relax, the stiffness leaving his shoulders. I wondered how many times Steve had left Linda alone in her bed, pulling away as soon as his climax was over, avoiding the gentle arms that threatened to draw him close.

"Are you sure you can't make it at the weekend?" Margaret said over the phone.

"Sorry ... " I felt guilty for hurting her. "I'm staying in revising. First exam next Monday and the last on the Friday after. I can't believe it will be over so quickly."

"Don't you think you could do with a break from your books?" Margaret said quietly.

"I must press on."

"Perhaps after the exams are over we can meet. We'll have loads of free time, Martin."

"Yes," I lied. "Perhaps then. Take care."

"And you."

I could hear the quaver in her voice and something within me shivered.

"Bye, then." I put down the phone.

I read through my notes on Gladstone and Disraeli for what must have been the hundredth time. I was sure I was going to get it all muddled up tomorrow in my first three-hour paper.

Candidate 107.

I thought of us all sitting there in the dead quiet, row upon row of small square desks strategically placed three feet apart so no one could cheat. The papers face down on the desk as you went in armed with only a pen and pencil, straining your ears to hear the instructions the invigilator was giving you, keeping your eyes on the clock and the blackboard with the finish time chalked on it in huge white letters. Everyone would be glancing around them, smiling nervously, trying to pretend it was all a joke. There would be the rustle of two hundred of us simultaneously turning over our exam papers, and then a peculiar silence would descend as we bowed our heads to the task in hand.

Mum came in the front room and gave me a worried

look.

"Don't you think you should stop now," she said, softly. "It's getting late, love."

I looked up from the table strewn with file paper.

"Just Palmerston's Foreign Policy, and that's it," I told her.

"Dad says it's silly to cram," she told me, hesitantly, one hand straightening a fold in her dark green skirt.

I took no notice.

"Are you nervous, love?"

I faced her, responding to the gentleness in her voice with the truth.

"Yes, I am. Exams always scare me."

I reached out and took the hand that rested on her hip and squeezed the bony fingers quickly. For once Mum didn't move away. Instead, she stretched out her free hand and stroked the hair back from my forehead.

"Your big day tomorrow," she said, quietly.

I nodded, keeping my eyes on her, savouring the peaceful moment between us that had come out of nowhere, and made words redundant. We could be friends, Mum and I. We wanted to understand each other.

Then I remembered she knew nothing about what I felt for Richard, believing only in the relationship with Margaret that I'd masqueraded before her. A sense of separateness, of being entirely on my own filled me and, cold inside, I let go of her hand and returned my gaze to the papers in front of me.

Dad threw the white envelope within my reach. He hesitated, waiting for me to open it and I paused, yawning, waiting for him to go and leave me alone.

"Make sure you do all the questions," Dad said. "And don't rush anything. Take your time."

"I will."

"Keep your eye on the clock."

I nodded my head, my hand stretching out for the envelope, turning it face up so that I could see the handwriting. I recognised it at once.

"Good luck, son."

"Thanks, Dad."

"You'll do fine ... "

We looked at each other, our eyes meeting and for a moment I saw how tired and vulnerable he was inside. It was like seeing into a dim room that was cold, without light or fire. Only there was a thin figure sheltered in the gloom, afraid to move either forward or backward. He could only stare with beseeching eyes and wait for help. I wished I was able to move towards him as Mum could. I wished I could offer him some warmth, but he always turned away from my reaching arms as if he was afraid of my touch, afraid that he was a man at all, someone who needed other people.

Then he walked away, his footsteps heavy on the stairs. I heard him call out to Mum.

I picked up the letter and stared at it, forgetting about Dad, aware of the sunlight streaming in through the window. Ripping open the envelope I pulled out the Good Luck card, and sure enough, inside was a message from him.

All the best. Thinking of you.

Richard

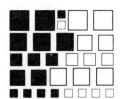

10

My exams were finished, school was over, and I'd walked out of the school gates for the last time. I felt happy, I suppose. All those weeks of work were behind me. I could forget about Forster, Chaucer and Auden and British Foreign Policy from 1850 to 1914. I didn't need to burn my books, it was enough that I wouldn't have to look at them again.

I wanted to be free from school. The boy who had grown up there no longer existed in quite the same way. I wanted to bury Jumbo forever and discover who was Martin Conway.

When I thought of Richard, when I gave my feelings freedom, it was like I'd let a thousand birds out of their cages and, surrounded by the beating wings, I knew I was *alive*. If I shut that life away, then I could sleep with Margaret, I could use her like a doll that passively allowed me to take my pleasure without crying out. But I couldn't make love to her as a person. The only thing she'd asked of me was that I stayed, and I had left her.

Leaving school I faced an unknown world with unknown possibilities, a future whose blankness filled me with dread as well as anticipation. But even half-afraid, I still wanted to break my ties with the old world, and walk forward unashamedly holding the hand of the person I cared for. I was determined to be the young man that I truly was, and not some manufactured personality that lived up to others' expectations and denied my own real desires. I didn't want to pretend any more, to be a puppet pulled by other people's strings. I wanted to be free to be myself.

I didn't realise how hard it was to be free, to behave the

way you wanted to. The world prefers tidiness, it prefers everything and everyone to be labelled and put away in boxes. Free from school, feeling as if I was free from everything, I was determined to reach for what I wanted and wander where I pleased.

But it was only a matter of hours before the world changed again, everything arranged along straight lines that made no room for me.

First of all, Linda rang.

"You are going to the dance tonight?" she asked.

"Of course, I'm celebrating. Meeting Steve in the Weavers at eight."

"What about Margaret?"

I hesitated, unable to tell her what was in my mind. I was sure Richard would be at the dance. I wanted to meet him there. It had been weeks since we'd been together and yet I could still recall my longing, the rising desire to reach out and touch him.

"I'll see her at the dance," I said at last, and I sensed Linda hesitate at the other end of the line.

"You won't hurt her, will you, Jumbo?"

I felt guilty then, wishing I was on my own, that no one reached inside me, no one demanded anything, no one cared.

"I can't ... " The words stuck in my throat.

"Jumbo ... " Linda began, but I interrupted her.

"I'll hurt Margaret as little as I can," I said quickly, and there was a pause while Linda realised what I meant.

"You haven't been seeing Richard, have you?" she said.

"No ... I haven't. I've been busy. Exams and every-thing."

"I told you to forget him, Jumbo," Linda said gently. "I told you ... "

And then I put the phone down. In the silence I could hear Linda's words repeated over and over again inside my head. The hopes of freedom disappeared, the memory of my ideals mocked me, painted me a clown's face, frozen in my mind with a sickly grin, the helplessness dark in the brightly made-up eyes.

Margaret hovered at my side like a ghost that wouldn't go away.

"Let's dance, Martin," she said.

"I can't. I'm clumsy."

"I don't mind." Her hand lightly touched my arm, but I didn't relax.

"I look ridiculous," I protested, and she turned her gentle eyes to me, not understanding.

"Please ... " she said, helplessly. I wanted to remove her hurt, but my touch would only have confused her even more. I kept my arms straight at my sides and turned half-away from her, surveying the milling crowds in the bar.

"I'm going to get another drink," I said. "Want one?" It seemed all I could offer her.

Margaret shook her head, the disappointment dimming her eyes, and then lifted her face to me again.

"Haven't you drunk enough?" she said.

"It's celebration time," I told her. "End of exams. End of school. End of everything."

I pushed past her, wanting to lose myself in the press of dressed-up young people, shining hair and painted faces, the smell of sweat and perfume thick in the air.

"Martin ... "

I ignored her cry, hating myself, and pushed my way roughly to the bar. Someone called me a rude bastard, but I didn't contradict them, intent on catching the barmaid's eyes. Another pint and I wouldn't care about anything, anyone. I paid my money, took a draught from my pint glass and then headed for a side door which led in a roundabout way to the garden where I'd found shelter before.

I was sure he'd be there waiting for me, a pale figure standing quietly on the grass surrounded by the dark, cumbersome walls of tree and hedge. But no one was there. I walked right round the garden, looking behind the tree where he'd been standing before. I even called out his name, but there was no sign of anyone.

It occurred to me for the first time that Richard didn't understand or reciprocate my feelings; that he, innocent to my desire, offered friendship rather than love.

I thought how much the truth would disgust him, how he would turn away, the revulsion bright in his eyes. There'd never be another letter from him, never another card, never anything.

I was a freak, I thought. No one would understand or love me. I wallowed in self-pity like a huge hippopotamus up to his ears in mud. Perhaps it was all the drink that did it, the alcohol that threatened to bring tears to my eyes.

And then I heard footsteps and all my fears were buried under a brimming wave of anticipation as he came walking towards me, a slight figure in the pale yellow trousers and red tee-shirt.

"Richard ... "

He looked startled at the sound of my voice, the emotion I'd betrayed in one word, and then he smiled awkwardly.

A silence left me empty, as if I was a lone figure standing waiting in a huge hall with a high, arching ceiling.

"I thought I'd find you here," he said, and turned his face away from me. "I don't know why I came. Silly, isn't it, when you don't want to speak to me."

I tried to tell him how wrong he was, but though my mouth opened and closed no sound came, and I saw him move even further away.

"Everyone tells me you're going out with Margaret Turner," he said, lightly. "Congratulations."

"I'm not going out with her." My voice shook.

"Everyone says you are." An anger crept into his voice. "You can leave me waiting in the pub, you can refuse to answer my letter, you can ignore me, but do you have to lie?"

"I'm not lying."

Richard turned and faced me then, and I was sure he hated me.

"Really?" he said coldly, and began to walk away.

"Richard ... "

He hesitated, turning back to me, but his voice was still hard.

"You called me back before, remember. Look where it got me. Nowhere."

"I'm sorry."

"So sorry you couldn't even write, couldn't even pick up the phone."

I stood there, uncertain of what to say.

"I wanted to ... " I began, and then my voice trailed off into nothing. For the first time I realised how hurt he had been.

"It just slipped your mind, did it?" he said, sarcastically.

"I was scared ... "

"Scared?" Richard turned round and took a step back to me.

"Worried," I countered. "I was worried, that's all ... " and then I was frightened that he would go before I could explain myself. "Don't go, Richard. Please. I'm asking you, all right. Please, stay."

All the hurt and anger was taken out of him, drained away by the emotion in my voice. I bowed my head, and when I looked up again he was so close to me I could have reached out and touched him. I felt his hand lightly on my arm and I shivered though the evening air was summer warm. Richard was closer still now, looking into my eyes, looking right inside me, aware of the stranger that no one else had ever seen.

"Why were you scared?" he said, and the gentleness in his voice called out to the stranger, called out to me.

And we both knew.

"I was scared of what I felt." My voice quavered, and I swallowed hard, anxious that he should understand. "What I felt for you scared me ... "

For a moment there was silence, but inside me it was like the vast empty hall was full of people, feeling, bustling everywhere, excited, burning like the flames of candles on a birthday cake.

"I was frightened too," Richard said, softly, and then his fingers reached up and traced a circle on my cheek.

Clumsily, I took his hand and clasped it tight, panic exaggerating the gesture, and he cried out. Immediately I let his hand go and turned my back on him, my face burning with shame. I felt so ugly I wanted to cry. *Jumbo. Jumbo.* I kept hearing everyone shouting and they were all laughing at me.

But Richard was quiet. His hands moved slowly up my back onto my shoulders and, gratefully, I let myself be turned round. He held my giant hands in his thin fingers and smiled up at me, looking straight into my eyes.

"There's nothing to be afraid of now," he said.

And at last I reached out, put my arms around him and drew him close. Resting my head on his shoulder I felt his breath soft against my ear. Aware of his body I drew him closer still, desperate for the peace I'd found in his arms. He trembled and I heard him sigh. He turned his face up to mine and we kissed, uncertainty giving tenderness to our embrace. As he slowly moved away, he took my hand.

"So I'll see you tomorrow?" he said.

"Yes."

Richard smiled.

"Let's go somewhere different. The seaside. Let's go to the sea."

"It's miles."

"We'll go early. I'll pick you up at eight. I can borrow the car for the day. My father won't mind. Please."

And then someone called my name.

For an absurd moment we looked at each other as if we thought we should hide.

"Jumbo ... " the voice called again. This time I realised it was Linda.

Before we could do anything she walked into the garden

and saw us.

"Hello," said Richard.

But she ignored him. Instantly, I was so angry at her snub that I wanted to strike her. The violence of my feeling appalled me. Linda stared at me unaware. Richard broke the awkward silence.

"Eight, then," he said brightly.

I nodded my head.

Richard smiled at Linda as he walked past and I saw the physical effort she went to not to shy away from him. She stood there like a waxwork doll and it was only as I moved to follow Richard that she came to life, stepping in front of me , her eyes alight with hurt.

"Jumbo," she burst out. "After what I told you. You promised me."

"I didn't."

"What would your parents think? Your Dad, your Dad would hate it, Jumbo. His only son a ... " Her voice faltered.

"Go on," I said, brutally. "Say it. His only son a queer."

"Jumbo ... "

"That's what you meant, isn't it?"

"All right!" Linda shouted. "I'm sorry. Maybe I can understand. But some people won't. However misguided they are, there are people that will despise you, that will want you put away. Your Dad, Jumbo, he'll want you sent to a psychiatrist. I know he's wrong, but he'll try and change you. He couldn't bear you to be ... "

"Bent ... " I offered. "Go on. Say the words. Say every single name you can think of."

"Jumbo, please ... "

"It's sick what you're saying," I shouted. "Sick. Perhaps it's Dad that needs locking up, Dad and the rest of them that don't understand."

"I understand," Linda pleaded.

"Do you? Look how you just ignored Richard. You treated him like he was shit."

"Jumbo, please ... "

"Please, what? Please go back to Margaret and pretend I'm normal, is that it? I screwed her, Linda. I screwed her just like any other man could. Are you satisfied? Does that make it all right, that I'm just like any other man? It doesn't matter if I hurt her, if I pick her up and have my fun and use her. It doesn't matter how many people I hurt as long as they think I'm a man."

Linda stared at me, the tears shining in her eyes, and strained her face to speak.

"I'm sorry. Jumbo, I don't think that. I don't. I care, whatever you feel we're friends and I care. Jumbo ... "

The tears ran down her face. I held out my arms and she came to me and held me tightly, shaking, the cries muffled against my shoulder. I stroked her hair and patted her back like she was a frightened child that needed comforting.

"I'm Martin Conway," I murmured over and over again. "I'm Martin Conway. Martin. Linda, you must understand."

The sobs subsided and there was quiet. We said no words to each other, but something in both of us made us refuse to let the other go.

I walked Margaret home that night, taking quick strides, avoiding the touch of her hand. I was too full of feeling, too uncertain to speak with her and so I kept my silence, holding my secret inside me, burying my hands deep in my pockets.

"Martin ... "

I ignored the crying sound in her voice until we stood apart from each other on the path outside her home.

"You could come in, Martin," she said, quietly and reached for my hand.

I took a step backwards from her.

"I'm being a bastard ... I'm sorry," I said, managing a feeble smile.

"Don't you want to see me any more?"

I closed my eyes to the hurt in her voice, and my silence answered her question.

Margaret turned away and I knew it was impossible for me to comfort her.

"We can be friends still ... " I began, and then my voice disappeared into nothing.

"I want you ... " Margaret said in a wavering voice.

"I'm sorry." I half-reached for her arm then, but she pulled it away from me and stood there stiffly like a person someone had turned into ice.

There was nothing I could do now.

Slowly, I put my hands back into my trouser pockets and turning, without another word, began to walk away.

I stood in the hallway, feeling sure that he wouldn't come, my eyes checking the wristwatch that said ten minutes past eight.

"He's late," said Mum, still in her faded pink dressing-gown. She handed me a package. "Something to eat," she said. "Cheese and tomato rolls. You could put them in the bag with your swimming costume."

A quarter past eight.

"Don't fret, love. I expect he overslept."

I smiled at the gentleness in her voice, and felt my shoulders relax. Reaching out, I squeezed Mum's hand. She held onto my fingers and we looked at each other, sharing a precious moment of peace, before she let go.

At the sound of footsteps on the path I was as nervous as a baby. Mum scampered up the stairs for the sake of decency, determined that no visitors should see her in her dressing-gown.

"Have a good day," she called.

"Thanks."

I opened the door and there was Richard standing there in blue jeans and a pale blue sweater.

We both wanted to touch each other then just like any other young couple would, but the conventions we'd grown up with restrained us, kept us apart like dolls on strings. I flushed and picked up my bag.

"The forecast's rain," Richard said quietly. "Perhaps you ought to bring a coat."

"In the middle of June," I said, tutting like an old hen as I took my anorak from the hall cupboard just in case.

I put my belongings in the back seat of the green Cortina, and then seated myself in the front next to Richard. I was too afraid to look into his eyes, scared that the whole impossible day would go horrendously wrong.

"Relax," he said as I fumbled with a seat belt. He reached over and touched my arm and I turned, met his gaze, and knew everything would be all right. I'd seldom been as happy as I was then, with him close to me and the prospect of us spending the whole day together.

The roads near the promenade were jammed with the cars of holiday-makers, most of whom were sheltering in their hotel and boarding-house rooms. Rain fell from an iron grey sky in thin misty showers and a few dripping holiday-makers struggled along the streets, pulling their restless children behind them.

The Amusement Arcade on the pier was packed with people of all ages, shoving money into machines that whirred and jangled, flashing tempting lights before disappointing the daytime gamblers. We took a look inside and then retreated back into the fresh air and the drizzle that dampened our hair and left our clothes moist to the touch.

Everyone around us seemed glum and bad-tempered; a woman yelled at her young children and two elderly people looked at each other with worn faces and found nothing to say. Most of the holiday-makers couldn't find time to smile. Some leaned over the pier rails, staring mournfully out to sea as if they wished they'd decided to risk it in sunny Spain.

Richard stared down at the waves crashing onto the shore beneath us, white water breaking round the black rusty rails that supported the pier. Above us the gulls, with grey black-tipped wings and white faces, wheeled and circled, crying out hoarsely to one another before swooping down in a flurry of wings to settle on the waves. We watched them bobbing up and down like grey floats.

"It's funny, isn't it?" Richard said suddenly, turning his grey eyes towards me.

"What is?"

"Us. You and me. I never thought that you'd like me. You do like me, don't you?"

I nodded, wanting to reach out and take his hand, but two old people were standing next to us, and I was afraid of being seen joining fingers with another man. My fear annoyed me, and Richard glanced at me, questioning the anger that crossed my face like a cloud.

"What is it, Martin?"

"Nothing."

"Tell me."

"We can't touch." I even found myself lowering my voice. A breeze swept my words away like useless bits of paper and I knew Richard hadn't heard.

"Martin ... ?"

"Let's go somewhere quieter," I said, loudly. "Away from the people."

Richard nodded, understanding.

"It's a long walk," he said, "but there's a beach along the far end in front of a field that's never used. Especially today with the rain."

"I'll follow you," I said, and again I wanted to take his hand. It was such an easy thing for a boy and girl to do without thinking, without having to worry what anyone else would feel. I wondered if it would always be like this, always the worry of what other people would think, always having to hide my feelings.

"Cheer up," said Richard. "I'm here. Remember."

For the tiniest moment he rested his hand on my shoulder, it might have been a brotherly pat, and then he turned away and walked through the thin trail of people wandering along the pier, wrapped in their macs or sheltering beneath umbrellas.

The beach was deserted. Richard ran down the slope that would hide us from anyone's eyes and jogged along the shore, teasing the waves with nimble feet that avoided getting soaked. I followed behind him, keeping my distance from the breaking waves, knowing I would end up wet-socked if I played the game. I wondered if the nickname Jumbo would stick at the college in Hull, when I'd be slow-footed on the tennis court and the football field. But September was miles away. I told myself that all this summer there would be me and Richard.

"Dreaming," Richard called out. "Dreaming, Clyde?"

"Clyde?" I shouted back.

Richard retreated from a wave and then half-fell, half-sat back on the grey blue pebbles on the beach.

"Your new name," he said, turning and smiling at me. "Clyde. Do you mind?"

"No ... I suppose not."

"I don't like 'Martin'."

"I hate Jumbo more. Martin's all right. But Clyde, what made you think of that?"

"You're big and gentle. Someone called Clyde should be just like you."

"It sounds like a cart-horse to me ... I don't mind it, though."

I sat down awkwardly beside him, and we looked at each other, uncertain of touching.

"Big and gentle," I said. "Is that what you think?"

"Well, you're over six foot, aren't you? You dwarf me."

"And gentle?"

Richard looked at me quickly.

"You shouldn't get a complex about that," he said. "I don't think you're weak at all. Gentle is a compliment."

"Not for a rugby player." I smiled uneasily.

Richard's face stayed serious, and for some reason I held my breath.

"But you're a person first of all," he said. "Everyone should be *gentle*. It means you have a caring respect for other people. It's nothing to do with soft."

The firmness in his voice somehow intensified the feeling between us and, as we looked deep into each other's eyes, I felt his hand grazing my face. Slowly, he drew my head towards him, and we kissed lightly.

"Well ... ?" he said. "You look surprised."

"I expected it to be different."

"Different?"

"From kissing a girl. It feels the same."

Richard kissed me again, only the moment was longer this time. A surge of feeling filled me and my hands took hold of his shoulders and held him close. It seemed the most natural thing in the world to do and, as we drew apart, I laughed because suddenly I was no longer afraid.

"It's better," I said.

"That's because you care," he said, quietly. "Perhaps you didn't care for the girl."

"I liked Margaret ... " I began and then I flushed, embarrassed.

"Liking isn't quite the same, is it?"

"No. I want you." The words came with difficulty and Richard's fingers smoothed the lines on my face away. I took his hand and held it tightly.

"And Margaret?" he said.

"I slept with her, but afterwards ... it was awful, like it was nothing. I didn't want to touch her."

"Does she know?"

"That I'm homosexual?"

Richard frowned, and then turned away.

"I don't like that word," he said. "It's a term, a label. Don't you think you're more than that? Don't you believe you're a feeling person?"

"Of course."

"Then there's no need for labels, is there? We're all people, Martin, whoever we fall in love with."

There was a silence.

"But if I'm in love with another man ... " I began, awkwardly.

"Then that's all you are. In love with a man. Love doesn't stop you from being a person. It helps you be a better human being. No one is totally male, Martin, or totally female. We're a mixture of both; a part of Mum and a part of Dad. Everyone is. Everyone has feelings towards someone of the same sex, whether it's as a friend or as a lover. In some people these feelings are stronger, that's all. A particular person might bring certain feelings out."

Richard hesitated.

"The only man I've slept with was married. He even had two kids. He loved them. It tore him apart that he wanted me. He couldn't accept that that was just the way he was; he happened to be attracted to me. He slept with me, but that didn't make him homosexual ... But he wanted to fit, Martin. He wanted to fit himself in a stupid box with a foolish label. Only Homosexual and Married Man didn't go together. He almost cracked up ... So don't tear yourself apart, Martin. You're a person, that's what counts most of all. You're capable of caring for other people. Be glad of that. Some people find it so hard to love. They're just motivated by desire, or what they think is desire, and they channel it the way society believes they should, towards a husband or a wife. Society doesn't make room for people like him, for people like us."

He turned and looked at me.

"We make room for ourselves. With love."

There was a long, long silence. Richard stood up and walked along the shore, stooping to pick up a handful of stones that he cast one by one into the waves. After a while, I followed him, treading uncertainly over the pebbles.

It started to rain again. Richard stood and watched the waves rolling in. The rumble and rush of the foaming breakers was loud in our ears. I reached out and took his hand.

"I don't mind the rain," he said.

"I should hope not," I said. "Not with me holding your hand."

Richard laughed, and I moved closer towards him, reaching out my arms. He pressed his face against my shoulder and I shivered because he felt so small and vulnerable in my arms.

"Even if it thunders," I whispered. "Remember I care."

And suddenly he pulled away.

"But for how long?" he said, the uncertainty cutting into his face in tight white scars.

I wanted to reassure him, reassure myself. Everyone is afraid of caring. Everyone is afraid of being left alone.

"I don't know," I said, and then I realised I was scared too. We couldn't know for sure what lay ahead.

I reached out and held his hand. And I was happy. Wishing it would be like this forever. The sense of closeness, the shared delight.

He traced my brow with his fingers gently.

"We have today at least," I said, and smiled.

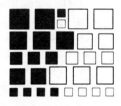

GMP publish a wide range of books, including fiction, art, photography, biography and poetry. Send for our catalogue to GMP Publishers Ltd, P O Box 247, London N15 6RW. In North America, our catalogue is available from Alyson Publications Inc., 40 Plympton St, Boston MA 02118, USA.